FLIGHT FROM OAXACA

DONNA HANELIN

FLIGHT FROM OAXACA

Illustrations by Yescka

MEDIUM SLOW

Oaxaca, Mexico

ISBN-13: 978-0-9960234-6-7
Book Design by Alan Pranke
Image Editing by Armando R. Freger

First Edition
PRINTED IN THE UNITED STATES OF AMERICA

THE HEALER

The plane that takes passengers from Oaxaca, Mexico to Houston, United States seats fifty. Seat A is to the left of the aisle, B and C to the right. I prefer to sit alone on the left. The double seems to connect you to a seatmate far more closely than on a larger plane.

There isn't much headroom. If you're over six feet tall, plan on slouching or indenting the ceiling. Forget about legroom. Even I, a woman of medium height, can barely maneuver. Still, it's my favorite plane ride in the world. Volcano tops, too tall for the sky, pierce the cloud cover. The coastal waters move from deep blue to inland seas of green. I always want to get out and go for a swim, but the great silver bird continues across the border, seemingly untempted.

On my most recent flight from Oaxaca to Houston, barely a month ago, I wasn't able to get a single. I was buoyed up for a double, though, excited at the idea of speaking English to an English-speaking stranger—something I had done infrequently during the previous months in Mexico. I was horny for English. When the young blond woman had to stand to let me take the window seat, I gave her a big smile, a hello, and a thank you. She smiled back, but her smile was mixed with red-rimmed eyes. Maybe she's tired, I reasoned. These 8:00 a.m. departures are meant only for the birds. Heaven knows what I looked like after a night of anxious tossing, turning, and peeking at the over-illuminated clock.

After the usual adjustments of baggage, purse, seat belts, and clothing, plane still on the runway, I stared out the window, reciting my silent, melancholy *hasta luego*, until we meet again, to Mexico.

"Look," I said, surprised to hear my own voice. "A swarm of big green dragonflies!" I sucked in my stomach and drew flat my chest as my seatmate leaned half over me to see what I had seen.

"I love dragonflies," she said. "In the pond behind our house, my sisters and I used to play games with them. We pretended they were fairies."

"Sounds fun." I said it without much conviction.

She laughed, but there was no sensation of humor in the air. "It wasn't exactly fun, it was pretty serious. My oldest sister, Kathleen, was crazy. I mean it, mentally ill, and she thought the fairies were controlling her, for reals. Sandy, my baby sister, and I played along—it was a good game, but later we found out she meant it."

"I'm sorry, that must have been difficult."

"Yeah, but still the dragonflies remind me of the simple part of being a kid." At this, a few tears fell. She brought out a damp tissue from her pants pocket. "It got a lot worse later," she said, as she dabbed her cheeks.

After a four-month stay in Oaxaca, not completely carefree, but released from my usual stateside worries, I wasn't sure that hearing English was off to such a good start. As often happens with jet talk, we were interrupted by the various safety and security announcements. I took it as the end of a chapter and figured we might begin on a new tangent after the steward had turned away from us and headed toward his own uncomfortable high-backed seat to buckle up.

For about fifteen minutes, as the plane took off and gained the proper elevation—in fact until we were well out of the Oaxaca valley and the clouds had come to block my view—it was quiet on our row 6, seats B and C. Then, I heard a sob arising from below the engine hum. I looked to see that my seatmate had probably been crying for several minutes.

When she caught my eye she said, "I'm sorry, but there was this man . . ."

"No need to apologize."

"I didn't know," she said. "I thought I meant more to him."

"Mexican?"

She nodded.

"I'm sure you meant a lot. It's not that. No doubt you meant everything. The problem is time. You meant everything, but not for the amount of time you had imagined." I caught myself, as I realized how cold I sounded. "Listen, I don't know anything about it. Not all men are the same. It's too easy to generalize. Meaningless."

"Naw, it's okay. He probably was just your average jerk."

"I doubt it," I said. "By the way, my name is Carol."

"I'm Lydia."

"*Mucho gusto.*" The Spanish in my mouth already felt far away and goofy.

"That was one good thing about it," she said. "My Spanish got a little better."

"*¡Qué bueno!*" A strange dull sadness came over me. I didn't want to hear about her man. I'd been on that aisle seat B myself, flying my way above and beyond a great love.

"He's a *curandero*," she said. "You know, a healer."

"Interesting." The truth is I wasn't particularly interested. In the California town I live in, every other person is a self-proclaimed healer. Once, a bagger at the grocery store offered me Reiki in the parking lot because I was upset at the rising cost of eggs. Anyway, *curandero* sounded better, but foreign words are deceptive.

"He learned from his *abuela*, his grandmother. She taught him."

"Herbs?"

"Herbs are part of it. He does massage and spirit cleansings. You might call him a shaman. He's very intuitive, he feels and knows. He knows energy. Sounds weird, huh?"

"Not weird, sounds like a heartbreaker," I said. "The one who feels and knows—isn't that the man we all want? Except he seems to know and *feel* everyone, and maybe we want him for our very own?"

"I did feel like he was all mine. You know, he was one of those people who, when they're with you, they're with no one else. I think each person was special to him, everyone mattered. I don't think he expected to be loved, but he was."

"He must be good-looking." The cynic in me is forever ready

to take over.

"I don't know about that. He's getting gray." She blushed, as she glanced at my hair.

"Oh well, darling, we all go gray. Nothing much to it."

"He seemed old to me, more like my dad."

"How old is he?"

"Fifty-five. I'm twenty-seven."

"You're right, he's old for you." I reached for the airline magazine I had flipped through months earlier on the flight into Oaxaca.

"Don't blame Macario."

"I've already read this one," I said and stuffed the tattered pages back into the seat pocket.

"I thought he was much younger, maybe forty. I had no idea!"

"Nice body?" I asked.

"Perfect, beautiful. He's a dancer."

"Such talent!"

"And a singer."

"And his wife?" I asked.

"How did you know?"

"Listen, sweetie, I'm not thirty-five or forty-five."

"What then, forty-eight?"

"I wish. Give me ten more years, fifty-eight. But the point is, a handsome, talented, and no doubt brilliant—"

At this she interrupted me to extend his range yet further. He spoke several languages, he had read widely—world literature, philosophy, psychology—and he truly was very smart. I shouldn't make fun of him, she told me.

"As I said, no doubt brilliant, fifty-five years old, and Mexican.

He'd have to be married, unless you had met him right after the most recent divorce."

"He helped me," she said.

"Good, I'm glad. Then he *is* a healer?"

"Sure he is. He cured a couple of friends who were having, I guess, emotional problems. I wanted to try it, a *limpia*. It's like a spirit cleansing. You see, five years ago my sister, the one I told you about?"

When I stopped hearing her voice, I realized I had turned my head toward the window again.

"You probably don't want to hear all this."

"Go on," I said. "But first take a look down there at the water." The ocean was the deepest, yet still the brightest blue I had ever seen.

After the obligatory peek, she said, "Pretty," then began again. "My sister, Kathleen . . . I guess one day the dragonflies told her to kill herself. Maybe it wasn't dragonflies. Our mother hates it when I say 'kill herself' instead of 'commit suicide.' She did. She shot herself in the head."

I gasped, but Lydia didn't hear. I thought only men shot themselves in the head.

"We hadn't been close for a long time. She didn't want me or my sister in her life. I think she talked to Mom sometimes. I felt really guilty about her suicide and angry. Macario knew as soon as he saw the egg."

"Egg, whose egg?" I was afraid we were going much further from center than I could manage.

She laughed. "Not whose egg, the egg. They use an egg to clean you."

"They?"

"The shamans in Mexico. They take a whole egg still in the shell and rub it all over your body and whatever is wrong with you goes into the egg somehow. Then they crack the shell open and drop the egg into a clear bowl of water, gently. They can read the egg in the water. I still remember exactly what Macario said. 'The sadness here is deep, and you must forgive a person close to you or you may have sickness in your lungs later.'"

"Sounds threatening," I said.

"I cried the way I did when I was six years old and went swimming into a swarm of stinging jellyfish."

"Is that it? You said he helped you."

"All that time when I was crying he held me, stroked my hair, and said, 'It's okay, *Chica*, it's okay, it's good to let it all go like this.'"

At this, she did begin to cry again in earnest, and though I was honored in one sense to receive her story, I also experienced the immense weight and depth of it. As she cried, I brought out a package of tissues for her, then closed my eyes in a fit of fatigue and drear. Hardly more than a minute had passed when, behind my closed eyes, a picture of this man, Macario, began to vibrate. What was in his words? Couldn't it be said of any of us: *sadness, forgiveness, possible affliction*? What more standard a verdict could any healer deliver?

"Thanks for this." I opened my eyes to see Lydia holding up the tissues. "I hope I didn't wake you up?" Her face and eyes were restored to a shine.

"No, no, I was thinking, trying to picture your healer, Macario."

On hearing my words, Lydia's story continued as if there had never been a break, as if no storm clouds had blown in. As if no rain had fallen.

"After the egg part, he rubbed wax over me, a votive candle without the wick. He said it was to remove curses, internal and external. Like if someone has done voodoo on you. The curse sticks to the wax.

"By then I was very weak. You know how it is after you cry? We were both standing through the whole thing. He was very close to me, I could hear my heart beating, and I was breathing more heavily than usual. He was too. I figured he had to, to do the work. He doesn't just skip around with the egg and wax. It takes a long time, three times all over the body. It's serious."

"Sounds serious for sure. You did say 'voodoo'?"

"He says the Cubans do it and since they live in the United States now, it's possible to get cursed without knowing it. He told me he had been to see a man who does voodoo in Oaxaca. Animal parts were stewing in a giant pot, and he saw dead human bodies in the back room. Macario sounded a little shocked himself. That was a relief to me," she said.

"Me too." I smiled at her. "Tell me, how does he know if you've been cursed?"

"He melted the wax in a pot on an electric burner, then poured the wax into a bucket of water slowly, until it formed a solid puddle. He said my wax looked fine, contained, except for one part that was sticking out, like Cape Cod, but not quite that narrow."

"Then you had been cursed? I hope not by a Cuban on Cape Cod?"

"You're making fun again," she said. "No, I haven't been cursed. He told me that part was my . . . this is pretty personal, my . . . repressed sexual energy."

"Join the crowd," I mumbled. She didn't ask for a repeat.

"But there was more, a sort of mark on the wax that looked like a smile. When I asked him what it was, he laughed and said, 'That's me.' Some more stuff happened. He showed me some exercises, I mean to help with the repressed energy."

As I envisioned the rest of this very, very old story, the words *holy shit* appeared in the clouds outside my window.

I almost called out to Lydia to take a look, but before I had a chance, she said, "I know what you must be thinking. It wasn't like that. He's not a bad person."

"What do I know? You said something about the average jerk."

"Did I say that?" She was a bloom of pure innocence.

"I thought so, but maybe I misunderstood. Something about meaning more to him."

"I'm confused about Macario," she said.

"I can imagine. None of us are one thing all the time, and the more you know of a person, the more confusing they are. My closest friends confuse me the most."

"I know what you mean," she said. "Anyway, he helped me, about my sister. It was the first time I faced her death directly. Since she died, I kept trying not to think of her, not to remember. I'd think about the many times she'd told me to get lost; it helped me to stop caring about her. But there were days when I couldn't forget how close we had been when we were kids, how she protected me from the bad fairies and introduced me to the good fairies. She always began with, 'I'd like to introduce my beloved, brilliant, but younger sister, Lydia.' Thinking of those words made me feel completely crazy. Fucking dragonflies," she said, then seemed to remember me. "Sorry, but ya know . . ."

I barely had time to nod.

"Fucking dragonflies. It didn't stop with the limpia. My shoulder hurt and I went to Macario for a massage."

"Is your shoulder better?"

"Sure, physical pain was nothing much for him—maybe it's like a real writer sending an e-mail, you know, a lot of talent for a little job. I don't think he took muscle aches very seriously."

"You're young," I said. "Those pains are harder to fix later on, even for a shaman."

"I guess, but it had been bothering me for a long time. Maybe a month. While I was lying on my stomach, he worked on my back and shoulder, and the pain was gone in about ten minutes. It hasn't come back either. That part was all pretty clinical. When I turned over for the second half of the massage, it changed some."

"Not as clinical?"

"When I flipped over, he was there staring at me. His eyes were intense, deep brown, almost black. He never stopped looking. At first I saw only Macario's face, but then Dad would appear and Kathleen and I'd want to run away from them, but those eyes kept telling me to go back to Kathleen. And each time I saw Macario, I was falling inside of him and running from him and toward him and away from and toward Kathleen and Dad all at the same time. I know it sounds awful, but it wasn't . . . because Macario was there." She stopped. "I kissed him."

Small blue dragonflies fluttered in my stomach. Maybe insanity ran in the family. But there was no sign of madness on her face, only a mild flush of excitement, eyes bright with love and more relief than agitation. The jet itself was more disturbed and bounced about in the cloud cover. This was nothing much for me. I'm a calm flier, but we were asked to stay seated and buckle up.

"I don't like this part," Lydia said, "when it gets bumpy." Even before she finished her sentence, we were flying smooth again, but it was a reminder that we weren't sitting flat on solid ground. "He kissed me back."

"I figured as much."

"The appointment was nearly over so it didn't get into a whole big thing. We just started talking like old friends. It was like he needed to talk. He's had a sad life. Seems like everyone he ever loved died. So many things had happened to him, worse than Kathleen. While we talked, I held his hand."

"Does he have children?"

"Three. They live with him."

"And he has a wife." I wanted to make a case for the fact that not everyone had died.

"Yes, and an ex-wife. Maybe two. It made me sad for him. I wanted to take the worry and pain away from him. He's such a kind person. I wanted to make him happy."

"That is part of love, isn't it? You know, he's lived a lot longer than you. More things happen the older you get," I said. "More happens, but it doesn't bother you as much."

"That's impossible." She sounded angry at me now.

"I'm sure it does seem impossible to you. The first death of someone very close opens you to all death. It's not that you won't grieve or that you won't be shocked, but death is not so far away. After the first time, you know it's a possibility. After a few more times, you know death is an inevitability. I suppose your friend Macario, being a shaman, has a good, close relationship with death. He may even have used death more than it's used him."

"What's that supposed to mean?"

Although I didn't want Lydia's anger, it was better than the weeping. I can't say why.

"He's made a career of it, hasn't he, helping people, as he did you, see the other side, the side of death, of darkness—the thing you had never faced directly? He's probably doing pretty well. Nice house?"

"Very nice."

"Well-dressed?"

"Guess so. He looks great in a white shirt."

At this point, the steward handed us each a lunch of shredded barbecued beef on white bun, accompanied by a cellophane salad. Though we were not delighted with the fare, hunger won out and a kind of pleasure took over aisle 6. Frankly, I thought I had gone too far in my preaching.

"I think I fell in love with Macario. Maybe it hasn't happened to you, like that . . . I mean a complete stranger?" Lydia asked.

"I've been in love, even with strangers. I know it doesn't sound like it, but I do understand, maybe too well."

As usual, she ignored my comment and I was glad. Last thing I wanted was to tell my stories of love and lightning.

"You asked about Macario's house. I was never inside it, but his office is there, around the back. He has an amazing courtyard of banana trees, a pomegranate tree, and passion fruit vines around the office door. Roses, too, orange ones as a backdrop for birds of paradise, and on one side, a hedge of yellow lantana. You could see a lot of the outside, even inside the office, but it was still very private. Dragonflies like the ones you saw before takeoff were there darting around a rock pond and lots of butterflies and those giant hummingbirds they have in Mexico."

As I was about to ask Lydia more about the plants (they had been a welcome relief), she picked up the love thread. "We kissed again, only this time I asked him, 'What do you feel when you do this?' I meant what is it like to be a shaman, but I didn't know quite how to say it in Spanish so it ended up being that same question I always ask guys: 'What are you feeling?' And he said, 'I feel what you feel.'" Lydia stopped to adjust her seat a half-inch forward. "What do you think he meant?"

"What do *I* think he meant?" I said it back to her in a daze. I was doubly tired from both the early wake-up and the density of her demand. When the steward came around with the coffee pot, I raised my cup to him like a beggar pleading for more time aware and alert.

"Do you think he meant he was in love with me too or that he felt whatever I was feeling because that's what those people do or do you think he meant—"

"Honestly, I have no idea. I wish I could be of more help, but I've spent a lot of my life trying to translate the statements men make in intimate moments. I decided a few years ago that either I'm a lousy linguist or it's simply not an interpretable language. And in all fairness, I doubt what we say makes much sense either. After all, what do you *think* he felt?"

"I hadn't thought of it that way."

We sat in silence again. I resumed my position as guardian of the skies, making sure all the clouds were enjoying their day, checking below on the condition of the waters, satisfying myself that the clouds still had shadows floating happily in the cupped palms of the ocean. And truly I was hoping Lydia would tell me more about the healer's garden, which interested me more than the man himself—a handsome fellow with a strong pair of hands, dark eyes, and an expendable conscience.

Lydia reopened the door to talk in an unexpected way. "What was it like for you?"

"What?"

"When you fell in love."

I shrugged. "Same as for you. I wanted him to be happy, I didn't notice that I wasn't happy, I believed the unbelievable, I translated the indecipherable, I ignored the ethical, and I had the time of my life." I corrected myself, "Times of my life."

"It happened to you more than once? Like that?"

"Yes, more than once. It began when I was seven years old and falling in love has continued for all the fifty-one years since." The revelation shocked me at least as much as it did Lydia. It wasn't even too far from the truth.

"I feel so crazy. Did you feel crazy like this, every time?"

"Probably." I suddenly felt very young, a small child lost in the garden of love.

"Didn't you want it to stop?"

"I don't know." I could see the trellises of white roses high above me, the rust-brown tiger lilies standing eye level in their beds. "I don't know. Do you want it to stop? Now . . . with Macario . . . or do you want it to continue, despite all the complications of distance, language, and marriage?"

"It has stopped." She said this softly and with great sadness.

"Seems like it's still going on, inside you."

And again she asked me, "Do you think so?"

"It's just that you've told me the whole story."

"No," she said, "there's more."

At that moment, the steward announced that we had to buckle up, the plane was beginning its descent, and in another twenty minutes we'd be landing in Houston.

"The time's gone by so fast!" I said, and I thanked her for her company.

Then she repeated, "There's more. I didn't tell you the end of it, the reason I know it's over."

"It's good, if you know for sure it's over. It's easier on the heart." I didn't expect she'd want to tell me the end. We didn't have much time, yet true to form, she continued undaunted.

"A week later, we went into the *temazcal* together, both of us wearing nothing but white sheets. At first I kept thinking to myself, 'What am I doing here alone with this magic man in a hole in the wall?' and I almost ran out. It's hard to explain. I know it doesn't make sense; I always felt safe with Macario. The temazcal is like a cave. He called it the 'womb of the earth.' And inside the cave there's a fire and steam. It's very hot and you sweat a lot. Every few minutes he threw water on the hot stones and the steam made more heat, more sweat. He called in the spirits by chanting and playing a kind of whistle. It was sort of boring, or maybe relaxing.

"After that I don't remember much of him or the womb of the earth because I had traveled five years back to the morning I went to the pond. I was visiting Mom and Dad after a summer of travel. They wanted to hear everything and assure themselves I was doing okay.

"The pond is below the orchard on their property, pretty far from the house. You can drive to it from the main road or just walk on a path through the fields and a corner of the woods. That's where my sisters and I used to play. We made our house in the forest, then would go talk to the fairies. Their home was the pond, according to Kathleen. I always walk down to the pond when I visit my parents. It's a special place, you know what I mean?"

"Yes, I think I do."

"On the way down, I found a bird's nest. There were eggshells in it, beautiful pale blue shells all broken, but the nest itself was perfect, round. I wanted to take it back home, but I knew Mom would worry about lice. I set it next to one of my favorite oaks and told myself to remember it. I'd get it later, right before I left. It wasn't until then, five years after, when I was in the temazcal, that I remembered the nest. I wanted to hold it again. When Macario took my hand, it felt like I had picked up the nest. I began to cry and he kept chanting. I once again forgot about him and where I was in real life.

"That day at my parents started out overcast. It was the beginning of fall, though it could have flipped back into summer— you know that uncertain time between seasons?"

Though Lydia was lost in her own story, she would still now and then stop to ask me something. At first I tried to answer, then realized the questions were part of her pattern of connection, not real questions. With only a few minutes until arrival, I knew I had better keep quiet. After we landed, I'd have to hurry to catch another plane.

"As I approached the pond, the sun was breaking through the clouds. I saw something floating at the edge, a log maybe. The sun shone right there. Though there were dragonflies flitting over the water, there was an especially thick concentration of them around that log. Perhaps the nymphs had just come out, but it was the wrong time of year. Then, too, it wasn't just one kind of dragonfly, but the big gold ones, the green ones, the medium-sized red ones, even the little blue ones. I'd never seen anything like it, the way the air shimmered."

My seatmate's story made me queasy. Even though I was sure of the ending, the anxiety wouldn't let up.

"Next I noticed a red tint to the water around the log. I kept walking slowly to the pond because I didn't want the dragonflies to leave. I wanted a chance to look at them up close. But each step I took made it clearer—it was not a log in the water. When I finally understood it, I ran to the shore, and there was a body—my sister, my Kathleen. I must have screamed out in the temazcal because I heard Macario's voice. 'Do you need to come back, *Chica*?' I remember shaking my head. I was in two places. In the womb of the earth and out by the pond. My heart pounded for Kathleen and for Macario all at the same time. But it was just like before. I wasn't afraid because he was there. I went back to the pond in my mind; this time, Kathleen wasn't dead even though I could see where the bullet had entered her head, and the blood was still there. She was standing up and we hugged. Her body was dry, and she told me not to worry. She said she was much happier. Then Kathleen asked me to go back home and leave her alone with the fairies. She said it exactly the way she did when we were little kids."

For the first time on the plane ride, Lydia had a smile of joy on her face. Though she had struck me from the start as attractive, she was now positively beautiful. I was the one with red-rimmed eyes. She gave me a tissue from the packet I had given her and apologized for such a heavy story, though reminding me it was a good ending.

"After the temazcal, I wanted to see Macario again. I really loved him, you know? I asked him to visit me. I wanted to touch him before I left Mexico, and I had so many questions about what had happened in the temazcal. It was like magic. How could I have seen all those things? He said he was busy with his family but be sure to call him if I was ever in Oaxaca again. That's all he said. That was the end of it."

Before we parted, I told Lydia I was happy for her because she had been able to see her sister Kathleen and to hug her one more time.

Then, to stop me racing toward customs, Lydia put her hand on my forearm. "What do you think of Macario?"

I had little time to consider. "I'm sure he cares about you, but love takes many forms. Before long I think you'll understand what happened. *Adios, mi amiga.*" I touched her hand, then proceeded alone into the bright and open Houston airport.

THE FAT DANCER

Strange how good we are at believing our own private reality is the all-pervasive reality.

Back when I first met my friend Marge, when we were both middle-aged, single women and she had retired to Oaxaca, she worked to convince us of the peace and happiness inherent in solitude. Now, at age sixty-seven, she was suddenly married. And I was to be airlifted to a higher plane of reality, which was distinguished for its thrill and joy of companionship.

"I'm sure," Marge said, "you'll meet someone very soon. You'll be happier." She gave me a table sculpture of a man and woman dancing, which had been a gift to her from the remaining spouse of a happily married couple. Now that he, too, had passed away and Marge had married her prince, Robert, it was time to send the dancers on to their next mission—me. I set the dancers, two figures carved from one solid block of wood, next to my leather bound edition of the world atlas. If this chunk of wood was a talisman, I reasoned, it didn't matter if I believed in it or not. After all, magic is called upon to overcome the slumps and shrugs of the nonbeliever.

Now I was heading back to Oaxaca to visit Marge and to meet Robert for the first time. I had decided I would not get into conversation on my travels south. The previous flight back home had been too wrenching.

Aside from a few words to a mother also waiting to board, I did keep to myself. In the mother's case, I couldn't help but admire her beautiful, plump baby boy who waved his arms and legs like a newborn butterfly fanning in the sun.

"*Como una mariposa*," I said.

She nodded politely. I blushed at having tried to be poetic with my Spanish "like a butterfly" and was relieved when the loudspeaker announced our flight.

On the plane, I read *The New Yorker* from cover to cover, including the theater schedules and wondered (again) why our fashion models had become peculiarly skinny and utterly unhappy. I don't know if it's stranger to see a full grin of perfect white teeth on the fashion pages or a stunning woman who appears to be surrounded by all the best in life looking as if she's just lost everything. I studiously avoided talking to the young man next to me, and he, too, seemed content to leave well enough alone.

By the time I arrived at Marge's, it was nearly eleven at night. All the plans had changed in the past forty-eight hours, but Marge hadn't wanted to trouble me with the news. Robert had gone on a quick business trip to the coast. When he returned, both of them would have to leave for the States to take care of Robert's grandchildren.

"Don't worry," she said, "you can stay here."

"But I came to visit you. And to meet Robert."

"I'm sorry, but we have no choice. His daughter just got divorced; we have to go help her. Rob will be back Wednesday afternoon, so you'll have a chance to meet."

We talked a while, the usual plane ride reportage, though I had little of interest to relate. I groused a bit more at being left alone unexpectedly until Marge finally let fall, "Things change, you know, when you're married."

I decided to ignore her insight, pleaded exhaustion from travel, and got into bed, both disappointed and irritable.

By morning I was more myself, that is, more like the better part of myself. It was difficult to remain disappointed when the brass band next door began practicing, pots of bright yellow roses were in full bloom on the patio, the mourning doves were making nests in the eaves, and the hanging laundry, like bodiless dancers, was swaying to a mild, warm wind.

"You look great. Did you lose weight?" Marge asked. We were having the first cup of coffee together.

I had lost weight. I hadn't been concerned with the shape of my body, which is obviously far beyond being well past its prime. What had interested me was how changes in the body had opened up parts of the character—how you can change emotionally by altering the positioning, the muscle, and the breath.

"It's possible I'm not the person I was when you first met me. The ways I've restructured my body make me feel like someone else, not at all who I was when we were both living here. You're a different person, too. Married, a new part of you has come to life, or you've found someone else inside the self you thought you knew. In a sense, you and I are like strangers meeting for the first time, seatmates on an airplane. You're now the married woman, and I'm, hell, I don't know who I am."

Marge laughed and reminded me of how dramatic I can be. There was no need for it. Yes, people change all the time, but friendship is based on something else, certainly not the tone of our muscles. She was glad I was enjoying my exercise routine; she had started swimming again and found it improved her outlook.

Although Marge hadn't understood me, I didn't bother to explain while bacon shriveled in the frying pan and she whipped the eggs into shape. Shifts in character aren't necessarily welcome, maybe especially by close friends. I wasn't ready for her new "joy of marriage" life either. I poured us both a second cup of coffee, set the table, and buttered the toast.

I enjoyed my few days with Marge. She had to make arrangements for leaving, but in between, we managed museums, restaurants, and markets. And several long satisfying conversations about the sense and nonsense of nearly everything. Aside from the usual new shops and cafés, the only thing different, and surprising, in Oaxaca was that the annual teachers' strike, usually lasting a few weeks during the least popular tourist month of May, was lingering into June. The tent city, normally contained around the central square, now seemed to be spreading a block or two in all directions from the *zócalo*. It turned out, something else Marge had neglected to tell me, that the day before I had arrived, the governor of Oaxaca had sent in the state police accompanied by one helicopter. It was rumored that a teacher had been killed. The city was in shock.

At home, busy with packing, I hadn't even glanced at the news. It's difficult to understand the mood of a place, never mind its politics. The character of the people is different in Oaxaca, outwardly tranquil and polite, making it tricky to fathom the depth of the unrest and pain. As Marge and I lightly floated in and out of tourist haunts, a political movement was taking shape block by block in the city, town by town throughout the state—a vital, earth-centered, and essentially peaceful force to ensure the rights and well-being of the people and lands of Oaxaca. And to oust an arrogant and brutal governor. For us, what was it? No more drinks in the now occupied zócalo, disturbed traffic patterns. How little we dared face the other reality!

A few hours before Robert was to return from the coast, Marge took me to a restaurant that specialized in corn. *Indígenas* made the tortillas there on the spot, just behind us. All the maize was from original stock native to Oaxaca. The food was delicious, the tortillas naturally sweet, but I was not enjoying the meal.

"Are you all right?" Marge asked.

"Actually, I'm furious." I couldn't stop myself from reporting what was old news to Marge. "People around the world, due to the genetic modification of seed, can no longer grow the grain staples from their own seeds. They have to purchase seed for every crop. And we have no idea what effect these modified foods will have on our health. Not to mention that the price of corn, now grown mostly in the United States, could rise beyond affordable for a majority of Mexicans."

My temperature kept rising. "Who are these people? Who is making these decisions? It's beyond greed. It's evil to modify a staple like corn. Corn is life for Mexico. Corn is Mexico."

"That's why I eat here. I do what I can." Her face remained calm as she spoke in a measured and practical tone.

I knew that Marge helped several grassroots organizations in Oaxaca. I was all blow and no action. However, I didn't appreciate my fury being reduced to the patronizing of a particular restaurant, an inaudible munching on protest.

We were nearly done with *comida*, when an acquaintance of Marge, a young Mexican man, walked into the restaurant. "Oh, there's Hector," she whispered rapidly to me as she waved at him. "He had an American father. And what a sweetheart! He helps us out at the orphanage."

He was an unusual looking man, twenty-five at the most, with dark skin, light eyes, and at close to six feet, a lot taller than the native Oaxacans.

After polite introductions, Hector grinned. "I'm celebrating my first anniversary today."

Marge looked shocked. "I didn't know you were married! Hector, those young women you've mentioned . . ."

He laughed and assured her he was not married. "I'm celebrating the first year of my life as a dancer."

Hector was large, not fat, yet not entirely solid. He had a hint of pride in his chest and a fluid grace to his movements. I wouldn't have thought he was a dancer, yet once the word floated above the table, he gradually began to morph into one.

"You've mentioned those dance classes," Marge said.

Hector looked at Marge with a touch of sadness, a slight furrow in the brow and downshift at the corners of his lovely eyes. "Yes, the dance class. And you, how is your new *esposo*, Roberto?"

"Robert is a wonderful man, so generous. But I'm not completely used to being married. You have to make a lot of adjustments living with someone else, and we don't agree about everything. It's not always easy." As she spoke her eyes were as bright as a five-year-old's shining at the first sight of a new, fluffy puppy dog. Though Hector and I nodded in serious understanding, I didn't buy it. It was clear Marge was thrilled with her new life.

"Stay with Hector and order the coffee flan for dessert. I have to go meet Robert. We'll see you back at the house. And Hector, Carol's a writer, so watch what you tell her." She was joking.

When Marge left, I turned shy. Hector was a stranger, and though he had graciously agreed to spend the time with me, I had little reason to think we had much to say to one another. I asked him how he would celebrate his dance anniversary.

"I was only kidding, but it is a year since I began to dance. I'm part of a class that's taught at the university. I'm studying to be a school teacher, but dance is very important to me."

"Salsa?" I asked.

"No, thank you, I have enough."

"I mean the dance, the class you're in. Is it salsa?"

"It's contemporary dance, I think you call it modern dance. My teacher was trained in the tradition of Isadora Duncan."

"When I was a little girl my mother sent me to dance class dressed in a tunic, just like Duncan's students. We used to hold long scarves while we jumped and leapt through space. I loved pretending I was a feather."

"I can picture you perfectly, floating like a feather!"

Now Hector was being too kind. Outside, I heard what sounded like a helicopter, though it might have been the 3:20 p.m.

flight coming in from Mexico City. Hector seemed to be listening also, but we both chose to keep quiet about it. I had no idea what Hector's politics were, and all my opinions were based on the liberal and agreeable notions of equal rights and justice that had been pressed into me from an early age in the northeastern United States. Of course I was "for the people," though here in Oaxaca I wasn't sure what that meant.

"My teacher studied in Paris when he was young with a woman named Yvette. He has a photo of himself with her. She's wearing a Greek dress. She had studied in Russia with one of Duncan's students. Sometimes we all get sick of hearing about Yvette, it gets to be too much! He must have been in love with her. Now we all laugh when he says her name and pat our hearts."

When I told Hector that my teacher curled her hair in tight ringlets that made her look Greek, he reached into his pocket and pulled out a woven band. He tied it around his forehead and though I'd never been to Greece, I was convinced he could hold his own in a vast plaza of deteriorating columns.

"Your teacher?" Hector's smile this time was one of all-abiding faith. He set both hands into a gesture of imploring, arms and palms open to the ceiling. Though a normal human would scrunch his shoulders up next to his ears to accomplish this, the dancer learns to keep the shoulders in place, even to pull them down some, to open the heart. Hector was perfect at it. "Did she look like this?"

The thought of my teacher, a grandmotherly Anglo woman, appearing at all like Hector made me laugh, and Hector, already clowning for me, joined in.

"She looked exactly like you," I said. "Except for her being forty years older, twenty shades whiter, about a hundred pounds lighter, and at least ten inches shorter!"

"Close enough," he said as he put away his headband. "You and I obviously come from the same lineage."

"I haven't been dancing lately, I'm sorry to say. Although I am cross-training, as one of my teachers calls it. I've shed the trappings of ancient Greece, wear gray sweatpants, and take Feldenkrais, Yoga, and Pilates classes."

Hector wondered if it wasn't confusing, keeping all the different modalities straight. I hardly knew what to say. It was no more confusing than the rest of contemporary life in the United States, where we ate food from all over the planet, flew wherever we liked, and drove cars pieced together from products made around the world. At times I thought it was wonderful. Soon we would understand one another and come together to save our earth; at other times I was overcome by despair, that nothing would ever be itself again and that while the rich could taste everything from everywhere, the poor didn't have clean water to drink.

"For me now, it's all I can do to keep up in this one class. I've already been through a lot this year." At that moment the serious, even sad, face I had seen earlier, seemed to settle in and become Hector. The sudden shift surprised me.

"You mean in the dance class?"

"Before I was going to the dance class, I was very depressed. The doctor wanted to give me medicine. Every day I had to struggle to make myself get up out of bed. I hated being alive."

"I'm sorry. Did something happen to you?"

"It started a long time ago. I think after my father died. I got very fat, even when I was still a kid. One day over a year ago now,

I saw my body facing me in a store window. I couldn't believe he was me. I looked behind me expecting to see a fat guy, but there was no one else on the street."

I wanted to stop Hector, to console him, but there was no room for my consolation.

And maybe it doesn't always help. Maybe we have to see ourselves now and then exactly as we are seen by others and not as we like to think we are.

"I was on my way to University. I had two more classes. When I got on campus, I saw two guys and a girl, about my age, all wearing headbands. Now and then they stopped to show one another dance steps. They were all very excited and concentrated. And I was hungry—I'm not sure how to explain it. My hunger changed. I was no longer hungry for food, I was hungry to be part of them, of their excitement, their lightness. I followed them to the theater, pretending I would walk into this other life. When I got there and saw the thin bodies in their tight dance clothes, I rushed away to my education class."

The flan had been set in front of me, and I took a bite; it was delicious, but I wasn't hungry, not for food, as Hector had said. I was hungry for his story and for his success.

"I was late for class. As I sat there catching my breath, I could barely breathe just from rushing. I realized what an idiot I was! Of course I could never be a dancer; in fact of all things I might be, this was absolutely the most impossible. You understand?"

"Perfectly. But when I saw you walk in here I said to myself, 'What a graceful man!' You must have had that grace even before you began the dance class. It's inside a person, not something trained into you. It's part of the whole rhythm and beauty of your life."

Hector was almost unable to speak. "You're too kind to me. A year ago I was a *gordo*, *puerco*, a fat slob. It's that simple."

Hector's "simple" hit me hard in the chest. "We all have difficulties, we all have things we want to change about ourselves, but that's no reason to call yourself names."

"It's the truth, though, that's how I looked. But when I saw the dance class, I changed. Almost overnight. I weighed thirty-six kilos more than I weigh now. I lived in hell, but I heard the strangest voice inside of me. It said, 'Do what you know you can't do. Dance!' I was close to happy for the first time in years.

"I had to wait two days before the next class meeting, and all the time there were butterflies in my stomach. I was afraid I might lose my resolve, that suddenly I would come to my senses and start to hate life again. So I knew I couldn't think about it, but I could think of nothing else." Hector's excitement faded a little, then he added, "It must sound stupid to you."

"Not stupid. Brave. It was much more than taking a class, but don't stop, please. What did the teacher say?"

"I thought the teacher would be a woman. Maybe a wish. Instead I was greeted by a handsome man, about forty-five, with his long hair pulled back and a band around his forehead. He didn't seem to notice my weight, just gave me a big smile of acceptance. He said there were only four other men in the class. And eight young women, some very pretty, as if that had anything to do with me. 'Girls never look at me because I'm too fat, I just want to try this out, okay?' I said to him. He told me I should give myself six months in the class and that there were other ways to get the girls. He winked. One year ago today. That teacher turned out to be someone very special. I have my life to thank him for."

"You were the one who decided to do this. You're the one who has done all the work. Maybe you have yourself to thank most of all."

"You don't understand. That man has loved me like a father. He has pushed and sometimes kicked me to go on, and he has protected me. It's not easy to explain. I always feel safe with him, even when all my muscles ache and I can barely breathe because I am working so hard in the class."

When Hector said he always felt safe with his teacher, I remembered Lydia from my last flight back from Oaxaca. She, too, had mentioned being safe with that man, a healer, though he had sounded to me (on the outside) quite unsafe. He had cured her somehow, had allowed her to face the death by suicide of her older sister.

Maybe it is this generation, our children; maybe they have a greater need to feel safe in a world we've laced with fear.

"What's it like for you, to feel safe?"

Before he answered, he looked at me as if I were a peculiar person, as if surely I must know. "Like nothing bad could happen to me . . . like you're a baby bird and not afraid to fly because there's a big soft net under you. Macario is like that, like a net. I've fallen and even hurt myself, physically and other ways this year, but something in his energy made me always believe I could keep going."

"Did you say Macario?"

"Yes, Macario."

"It's a common name here, isn't it?"

"Not too common."

"He sounds very caring."

"Caring yes, but more, he knows energy. He's a dance teacher and a healer."

"How do you mean? You mean, he says he's a healer?"

"He says he's a shaman."

"Last year flying home from Oaxaca, I met a young American woman who had gone to a healer named Macario."

"Lots of foreigners go to him. He gives them massages. That's how he makes a living. Dance teachers can't support a family."

"How big a family does he have?"

"He has three kids and a wife, a pretty recent one. His third."

"Then your Macario does sound the same as Lydia's Macario."

"Lydia, is it a common name?"

"No, not really in the United States, it's old-fashioned. A name older people have."

"Then maybe it's the same Lydia. *Lydia de caballitos del diablo.*"

"*Caba* de what?"

"You call them dragonflies, we call them the devil's little horses," Hector said.

"How do you know this, about Lydia?"

"I'll tell you, but I wonder more how you know!" Hector laughed. "Some nights after class, Macario and I go out for *cena*, supper. This one night it was raining very hard, toward the end of summer. He told me he had met a beautiful young American woman, Lydia. He had given her a massage and said she was surrounded by caballitos del diablo, your dragonflies. He was worried about her."

"But she hadn't told him. It was only something that happened to her later in the temazcal. After that, he wouldn't see her. He said he had to be with his family. She never told him about the dragonflies."

"Temazcal?"

"That's where she saw the dragonflies."

"She did one of those steam baths he does with groups of tourists? To give them a taste of indigenous spirituality?"

"She was alone with him. He helped her, maybe he even cured her."

"Cured? I don't know if that's the right word." Hector raised his eyebrows and gave me a big smile.

I was unsettled by this response, afraid I had sullied Lydia's reputation. I told him plainly, "They didn't have sex."

"Macario lives in the present moment."

"Maybe he does live in the present, but Lydia was living in the past."

"How can you know about other people? Alone in a room?"

It was foolish to argue with this young man I had just met about whether a young woman I also hardly knew had sex with a man I didn't know at all, but I needed to defend womanhood. Defend against what, I'm not altogether certain.

"I know because Lydia told me. Macario had opportunities to be with her, but he didn't take them."

Hector was still smiling and it made me angry. Are all men so single-minded?

"It wasn't an affair. He healed her of a particular pain. But I don't see how he would have known about the, what do you call them, diablitos? Lydia told me she had never had a chance to talk to him about her sister and the dragonflies."

"He saw her energy; it appeared to him as surrounded by dragonflies. He can see things. After I worked with him for a few months, he told me he had let me into the class, despite my size and lack of experience, because he saw butterflies around me."

"He seems to be obsessed with bugs."

"Bugs?"

"Bugs, it's another word for *insectos*. An informal word. Children use it more than adults."

"Got it. I remember bugs. It's a long time ago. When we lived in Arizona."

"So that's where you learned to speak English?"

"My father was from the United States, a librarian at a college in Tucson. He met my mother here in Oaxaca, he was twenty years older than her, but they fell in love. Maybe she wanted to get away from here. She doesn't talk to me about it. I know it isn't easy for women."

"I'm surprised she returned to Mexico. Wasn't she afraid to come back?"

"She was happy to come home. No matter how educated a person is—you have to meet my mother, she's a beautiful person, very smart and wise—people in Arizona treated her like a servant. Even people who knew she was married to my dad, it was almost like they forgot. I don't think most people wanted to hurt her, but she was never happy in Arizona, except alone in our family. Sometimes I was teased, too, threatened, twice beat up, by other children who didn't understand my dark skin. It was harder on me when we first returned to Mexico because I was a regular gringo boy, but with dark skin and no father."

"I'm sorry you and your mother suffered this way. It embarrasses me, that I live there, in the United States."

"We all live there. It's a place people make in their own hearts, a place where they exclude and fear other people. It's not just the United States, it's everywhere."

I wanted to sidle over to Hector and wrap my arms around him. Despite all he had seen, all the ways he had been shunned, he remained unjaded, pure of heart. I said a silent prayer that he would never change for the worse, that bitterness would run from him like hard rain off a clear, smooth window.

As my prayer ended, I heard a crowd of voices chanting in raggedy unison. At first I thought someone had turned on a boom box or music was starting up in the back room of the restaurant.

Hector put his elbow on the table, his head in his hand, closed his eyes, and shook his head as if to make the scene go away. "It will all come to nothing out there." His head still in his hand, Hector signaled with his chin in a vague direction away from himself. "More people will die."

Before I had a chance to speak, hundreds of people appeared on the street in front of us, some holding signs, some with arms linked. The ones in front were all women, dressed in traditional clothes. I commented to Hector how beautiful the women looked, many carrying bouquets of flowers. He glanced out, then adjusted his chair more toward me and away from the street. He didn't want to see. After the women, men came holding a paper and wire sculpture of a helicopter with a figure of the governor. Everyone in the restaurant was watching now, and the conversation inside grew louder. A few tourists looked frightened, some of the Mexicans were smiling evidently in sympathy with the cause, others looked irritated and after a while went back to conversing as if nothing unusual were happening. Though the voices outside were loud and strong, the march was not threatening to me. I had been in Oaxaca before when the teachers were on strike at the end of the school year. They always marched peacefully. This was by far the largest demonstration I had seen and from the looks of it, we weren't going to be leaving the restaurant anytime soon, unless there was a back door opening to an empty street.

"With so many people, something has to change."

"And at your demonstrations in the United States, the ones against the war in Iraq, has anything changed?"

"I think the Democrats will come into power."

"You think the Democrats will end the war or help Mexican workers or stop the torturing of prisoners?"

"They say they will."

"They all say they'll do this, they'll do that, they'll make a better world. Obrador says this also, but will he? Even if he could be elected president?"

"I can't argue with you. It's easy to imagine in another country things happen because of thousands of demonstrators. It's easier to imagine change in other places. Politicians seem unlikely to change the course of the world, even though they are perpetually altering it in one way or another. The real changes in human consciousness happen somewhere else. Maybe in the bodies of dancers."

"To dancers!" Hector held up his glass of melon water. I joined him, clinking happily. For a few moments I forgot the wars of the world raging beyond these turquoise restaurant walls and far away from this colonial city of cobblestone streets.

"To Hector, to his first year as a dancer!"

"You better look at me when we do this. Macario says if you don't look in the eyes of your fellow drinker, you'll have seven years of bad sex."

"I'd be happy for seven years of any kind of sex right now," I said.

"You're not married?"

"No, not married. I tried. Twice."

"Then you'll have to try one more time. You have to make three tries."

"Is that what Macario says?"

"No, that's what my mother says."

"Then to my third try, let's toast. *Salud.*" I looked him straight in the eyes, and he did the same until we were both nearly cross-eyed and giggling.

Though when I was a little girl I wanted very badly to be a grown-up, I have to say at that moment I desired to be thirty years younger. For the time it took to clink glasses, maybe Hector wished it, too. Then my feeling passed.

"You have a girlfriend by now?" It was a motherly inquiry.

"Yes and no."

"What part is yes?"

"Yes, a girlfriend, but there's a surprise." Hector looked at me as if to say, "What can I do? It's not my fault."

"There are four girls in the dance class who want to be my *novia!*"

"Ay, such problems! Do you have a favorite?"

Hector told me he was in love with a beautiful woman in his education class. He hadn't said anything to her. He had no idea if she liked him. He thought it was odd that he wanted this one woman when he easily could have had the women in dance class who were fighting over him.

"Have you talked to Macario about your problem?"

"He knows the problem. Not so bad for him because it's mostly foreigners who fall in love with him, a little stupidly. Then they leave Mexico."

"I'm afraid Lydia was one of those foreigners, who fell stupidly. You love him, too, don't you?"

"That's completely different!" Hector was put off. "I'm a man."

"You can imagine, though, if you were a woman and he had helped you the way he has, you might have fallen in love with him."

"I don't know. I'm a man and so is Macario."

"I'm a woman and I can tell you it's not so unusual for gratitude of this kind to turn into passion, and it doesn't mean there's anything stupid or wrong about the woman, not that she's easy or whatever you say in Spanish, but that she's a woman in her body, too, and feels gratitude not only in her heart."

"It's completely different," he repeated.

I noticed that Hector was slipping away again into his sadness, and I wanted to grab him before he let go and went into free fall. I truly respected the work he had done to change his life and had sympathy as well for the wavering in his happiness. I was sure that the woman in his education class, whoever she was, would come to love him. He only had to give her a chance and they would live together happily ever after. Such are the dreams I dream for others.

Out on the street, the march had nearly passed. A few stragglers walked by with their signs dragging, faces tired, and clothes rumpled with heat and sweat. I could hear sirens in the distance and hoped it was the response to a routine emergency, not the arrival of truckloads of militia.

"We better leave now," Hector said.

I agreed we ought to make a break for it.

"Would you like to come to the dance class? It's tonight at seven."

"I'm sorry, I can't tonight. I need to meet Marge's husband. It's our only chance before they leave for the States."

"Here then." Hector stopped to write his name and phone number on a napkin. "Call me when you want to see the class. Call soon."

I placed the napkin carefully into one of the myriad pockets of my traveling purse, knowing I would soon forget which pocket. I doubted I would go to the class. What would I do?

"Remember, you can dance with us. Macario likes visitors. And women, especially *extranjeras*."

"Thank you, but I can't imagine." Then I suddenly did imagine something. I wanted to tell Hector's story. "Would you mind if I wrote a story about you?"

"No, it's fine. It's an honor."

"And if I called it 'The Butterfly'?"

"No." He shook his head. It was quiet between us while he considered. "Call it 'The Fat Dancer.' You will?"

"If I have to," I said. I didn't like it as a title.

"You have to," he said, "because it's what's true. And something else. Tell everyone to dance!"

"Dance everyone!"

Dance everyone. I wish I could add to those two words the light in Hector's eyes, the open gesture of his hand, the lightness in his voice. As I strolled back to the house, my spirit was filled with his dancer spirit, making the air glisten and the ordinary appear magical. It seemed to me that everyone was dancing. No one needed to be told. The fruit vendors danced between crates of fruit, the taxi drivers danced on a stage of crisscrossed roads, and as I remembered it, the marchers danced in the light of monumental change. A light that shone everywhere in all our hearts, if only we could see it, if only we could bask in it, if only we could light the way to world peace!

Back at the front gate, after much fumbling with my new set of keys, I opened the doors to Marge and Robert's house. They sat together on the couch in the living room. As they danced in the warm, quiet, companionable light of married love, I was so overcome with loneliness I could barely breathe. I tried *Dance everyone*, but the words sounded hollow inside. I shed a few tears, in hopes that crying was also a form of dance.

I layered a smile over my tears, then headed toward Robert. "No, no, don't get up." He was tall and lanky with a long face—full of life, but not exactly spry. "I'm pleased to meet you," I said. "Marge has been so happy since your marriage. I've never seen her like this."

"Surely you exaggerate." He had a clear twinkle in his eye, which was the response I took to be the real one. Those few seconds gave me a glimpse of the solid ground of the friendship, as well as their true romantic love.

Marge added her modification, a flirtation, directed toward Robert. "I've been happy before!"

"Maybe I do exaggerate a little," I said, then told them about lunch with Hector. Though I went on at length about the march, I was careful to avoid the true depth of Hector's despair, his ecstatic love of dance, and his deep filial affection for Macario.

DEAD ON THE ROAD

It was about ten in the morning when the doorbell sounded. At my own house in the States, this would be no cause for excitement, but here in Oaxaca, staying at my friends' house, it was jarring.

I decided to ignore the ringing. I wasn't expecting anyone. It was probably the kids next door fooling around. I took my cup of coffee upstairs and settled down in front of the computer to make much ado about yesterday in the pages of my journal. I was writing about meeting Angela, an artist, who had photographed the recent mega-march against the governor. I had seen some of the march from the restaurant window with Hector.

Angela had been very welcoming. We spent a relaxing, and for me, informative, two hours discussing the art scene in Oaxaca. She showed me photos she had taken of the march—one so stunning

I can still see it now when I close my eyes. The image was of seven indigenous women handing bouquets of flowers to a line of policemen. Each man was protected by a transparent plastic shield and equipped with baton and gun. It looked like the revolutionary twist on an indigenous dance. The police couldn't help but smile at the beautiful young women who offered them flowers. Mere boys, they seemed to be standing there rigid through a terrible miscalculation of fate.

The march had not been as peaceful as I wanted to pretend. Angela told me that after she snapped that photo, she had to make a break for it. As the thousands of protestors tried to enter the zócalo, the police beat them down, randomly arrested close to two hundred people, and pressed back the crowd with water cannons mounted on trucks. A small group hurled stones and bottles at the police. It was suspected that these were out-of-state thugs hired by the governor to make the state repression look legitimate.

Absorbed as I was in writing down Angela's story, it took several loud shouts from outside before the name "Marge" penetrated my fog.

"Marge, Marge, are you there? It's me, it's Hector." The voice was urgent and anxious. Then there was more doorbell buzzing.

I rushed down the long staircase and worked my way through the two inside entry doors and the solid metal gates. I had secured myself to the limit the night before. Even from the inside, the double locks required a key. It was maddening. At home, I am used to no stairs and one unlocked door. People who know me walk in, then knock after.

When I finally got the last door open, an entirely different aspect of Hector stood in front of me, not the well-groomed young man heading to his education class. Now he was unshaven, pale, and sported dark circles of exhaustion around his eyes. He looked like he had slept in his clothes, too tired or preoccupied to remember to take them off. He seemed to have aged ten years.

I told Hector that Marge and Robert had left for the States, then, of course, asked what was wrong.

"*Mi mamá*. My mother." His voice slipped from anxious Spanish to depressed English.

I invited him in for coffee. He didn't have much time, he said, but seemed relieved to sit for a few minutes. His mother had been at the march but didn't come back until two days later. She was badly hurt. They had been to the doctor where she had received the necessary treatment, but something else was wrong.

I asked if I could help, though I knew it was a limp offer. What could I do?

Hector wanted me to go back to the house with him. "My mother always likes to meet people. It makes her happy."

He was grabbing at straws. Had I thought about it for more than two seconds, I would have told him that if she's badly hurt, the last thing she needs is a new acquaintance, but Hector looked so distraught, I didn't allow myself to think of all the things I would think about later. And by then, none of it mattered.

Hector told me that he and his mother often disagreed about politics. He didn't want her involved, but she was committed to the movement to oust the governor and to the idea, anyway (he had shrugged) of social justice.

"I didn't tell you when we were at the restaurant. I knew she was outside. I didn't want to think about it. My mother and I don't argue, only about this. And this time she assured me the march would be peaceful, the demonstrators were trained in nonviolence. Everyone agreed, his mother had said, that there would be no fighting." Hector shook his head. "Everyone, sure, except the governor. And the *militares*."

When he said she was safe now at home, I offered a "thank God."

"Is there one?" Hector countered, then quickly continued. "My mother was gone for two days. I didn't know where she was, then at night I got a call from her from a town northeast of here, far away in the Mazatec area. She sounded so awful, so weak, that my heart pounded with fear for her. She had been thrown out on the road somewhere, she didn't know where. She walked to the nearest house and asked for help, but they were afraid of the police. Evidently she wasn't the first person to be dumped in this region. Somehow she kept walking until she found people who weren't afraid. They brought her to their house—you'd call it a hovel—and tried to bandage her arm. They gave her *aguardiente* to help her relax, but my mother couldn't rest. She knew how worried I would be. Those Mazatecans saved her life. I don't think she would have survived much longer out on the road, though she says she knew she would get back to me. It wasn't that bad, she says. She still thinks of me as a little boy who can't hear the truth.

"Our doctor said she was lucky there was no more internal damage. Considering the bruising, he expected much worse. My mother has always been lucky."

Lucky? I kept the echo to myself. I suppose there are things we have to believe about our parents: unknown visitors make them happy; their children don't drive them to argument; and they are lucky. A terrible anger welled up inside of me, but it had nowhere to go, and stopped me in my path, like a blockade with tires burning black smoke at both ends.

I barely heard Hector when he said, "I shouldn't have let her go. She could have been killed."

"You're not responsible—your mother did what she believed in. You can't make these decisions for her."

He ignored my sage opinion, asked if we could leave now, and showed me out to his car, a VW bug. I'm always surprised when those old bugs start up and get me anywhere, but it puttered along in good form. Even though there weren't many cars, we moved slowly due to the remains of blockades and police directing traffic with a profusion of waving arms and random whistles at every corner.

In town, the streets were nearly empty of pedestrians, and I gradually noticed most businesses were closed, some even boarded up. I had hardly left the house in the past two days, and then only to walk and shop in my neighborhood a couple miles from the center. It was vacation enough to be writing and reading away from home and to see ripe mangoes and avocados spilling out of the corner vegetable stand. I was content to quit touring. Still, in the back of my mind, the tourist world of Oaxaca hummed, and when I wanted to join back in, it would be there, open-armed, smiling, stocked with *blusas, tapetes,* and *chocolate.*

Only now it seemed to be gone. The lower six feet of all the buildings were covered with graffitti strongly encouraging the governor to leave his post. Shop windows had been broken. Along the road, an occasional bus that had been used as a blockade was gutted and smoldering. I have to admit this scene excited me, the way the truth does sometimes, even when it is cloying and acrid.

The way, after a forest fire, you can see the true lay of the land.

"I've thought of returning to the United States. And taking my mother. I've had enough of all this." Hector pointed at the windshield, his finger describing an arc about equal to the one a wiper makes. "Last night when we talked, for the first time she said, 'Maybe we should go back to Tucson. Your uncle would like us to live there.' I've suggested this to her many times and she was always a rock wall. 'Go if you have to, but I'm staying here.' I wouldn't leave her alone and she knows it."

I listened to Hector talk about living in the United States and thought about how I talk of moving to Mexico. There's rage and outrage everywhere, all enveloped in the same undervalued atmosphere, all living on the same degraded earth. I wondered why I couldn't force myself to think of individual lives any longer, why I couldn't let myself imagine Hector and his mother happier in Tucson or me, happier or maybe unhappier in Mexico. I couldn't sort out the realities. Hector would have more money there. More money would be good. Hector's mother wouldn't have the rest of her family there. That would be bad. Maybe they would be safer? Hard to imagine. In Mexico, I would be in such a creative and vastly more wondrous place from my point of view, and it would be good. I would be horribly lonely without friends or family. That would be bad. None of the details added up. The world was at war with itself. In the end, I consoled myself. At least, I'm not in a real war zone. Or was I?

"You're thinking." Hector forced a smile in my direction.

"Maybe it's best to stay where you are and fight for a better life."

"You sound like my mother."

"I have none of the courage your mother has. My fight is all inside. Your mother has the guts to face the real enemy, as we say, the one of flesh and blood."

"She has too much courage."

We drove on in silence. Hector, I imagined, was swimming in his guilt and worry. I developed several different pictures of his mother: the friendly, the stubborn, the courageous, the frightened, the beaten. My suppressed anger morphed into a tickle of fear in my stomach. What if the police came to Hector's? What if they thought I was part of the movement? What if they deported, jailed, or disappeared me? All the wormlike worries about security crawled through my veins.

"Are you sure your mother will want to meet me now, when she's so hurt?" It was too late for the question.

"I hope so. A few days ago she was happy to meet anyone. Now, I don't know. I've put you in a hard position. I wasn't thinking. You sure you want to go?"

"I'm just a little nervous, shy maybe."

By the time the wave of shy terror receded, I noted the car had stopped moving. We were parked in front of a pink wall. I automatically reached for the seat belt to unhook myself. There was no seat belt. I reached down for my purse, then opened the door with a handle so small I could barely grab hold. I stretched up to a most welcome full-standing position, but my legs didn't feel very strong, which, I reasoned, was the effect of rumbling for forty minutes over bumpy streets in a VW Bug.

We were met at the door by Hector's aunt Rebecca who ushered us in. Before she shut the door, she glanced up and down the street, then double-bolted the door. The curtains were pulled across the windows; only narrow bars of light entered the kitchen.

"No one followed you here? I saw a van earlier up the street," Rebecca said.

Hector put his arm around her. "Relax, *Tía*, no one followed us, it's over now. Lots of people have vans."

After a nod from his aunt toward a closed door off the kitchen, Hector left and went to his mother. Rebecca offered me a drink. What I wanted was a double shot of mescal with a beer to cool it down but agreed to the ready cup of coffee. It was still morning.

We sat looking at one another for a few very long minutes. "I'm sorry about what's happened to your sister."

"Who knows what happened?" She sounded disgusted. "Lucia doesn't say. Except when she called here, when people up in the mountains found her on the road and helped her. She isn't even sure how she got there. She had gravel in her skin." Rebecca's tears pooled, but she wouldn't let loose one drop.

I could hear Hector talking to his mother, occasionally their voices rising up as if about to burst into argument, then returning again to a muffle. My discomfort in the kitchen formed as resentment toward Marge who had left me alone in Oaxaca with *her* friends. She should have been here, she'd know what to say and how to get the right kind of help. She'd be practical and energetic about the problem, she'd make decisive moves, she'd find a lawyer or a doctor or a candlestick maker. What the hell could I do? While I was still wishing I were a more dynamic someone else, Hector returned and said his mother would like to meet me.

"I told her you're writing a story about me. She said I deserved it. 'A long story,' she said."

We both laughed, the way we had back at the restaurant; that moment of laughter gave love and courage their needed place in my grousing heart. I set aside the fact that I had not yet started the story about Hector. All in good time.

Lucia was sitting up in bed. As Hector had told me, her left arm was in a sling. As I walked closer to say hello and she turned the right side of her face to me, I saw more of the damage—swelling with deep purple bruises and bubbly scabs. The left, unharmed side of her face was lovely, her one wide-open eye still shining with life.

Hector excused himself, saying he needed to go to the *farmacia* and also make a stop at Macario's office.

As soon as the door closed behind us, Lucia said, "Hector worries too much about me. He's a good young man, but in some ways, he's still a boy. There's so much he doesn't understand." She shook her head. "You have children?"

My fears dissipated almost immediately upon meeting Lucia. It helped that she was in no mood to dissemble. The trauma she had endured didn't leave either of us with an interest in mere politeness. Besides, what were we? A perfect duo of women who had enough in common to initiate the search for more in common. Hector was the start, now my child would be added to the mix and I supposed, before long, the rest of the world would become grounds for talk.

"I have one girl."

"They're harder than boys?"

"I don't know, she's the only child I have. Maybe a mother worries more about a girl than a boy. So much can happen to a girl, but she's grown now, nearly thirty."

"I worry about Hector, too. He's had a hard life. My husband died ten years ago. He was a very good man and a good father."

The fire in Lucia burned brighter. "Thank God he's not alive to see me now. It would kill him to see me like this. Maybe my son's right, it's all a big mistake." She reached over for an icepack on the table by the bed and held it against her swollen cheek. "Tell me about your girl."

I gave Lucia the short answers. No, she wasn't married, yes she wanted to have kids someday. We talked more about our children, the difference between raising boys and girls. We both bragged some, relishing our children's innate gifts, though I think I was doing most of the talking. Lucia seemed content to listen. I told her that even though I was divorced, her father and I had remained friends. Lucia said that kind of arrangement would be unusual in Oaxaca.

"The men here . . ." she began. "I'm sorry, it gets difficult for me to talk. My mouth is sore from . . ." Once again she stopped.

I offered to get her something to drink, but that wasn't it, she said, the soreness wasn't thirst. "Those bastards."

I'm not sure bastards is the right translation. It may have been more like fucking assholes, but in any case, I started to tremble as I asked her, "Who, what bastards?"

Rebecca knocked on the door, and Lucia called her in. She was going home for a couple hours, but she'd be back later with comida. Rebecca also reassured me that Hector would return soon, but I had a feeling his visit with Macario was going to take some time. We gave a round of light kisses good-bye, Lucia asked Rebecca to leave the bedroom door open, and then turned back to me. She didn't begin again until she heard the front door close.

"Rebecca is my youngest sister. Growing up, I was her little mother. I still feel like I'm her mother, even though she has a child of her own. I don't want her to worry. My friends, the people at the march, they probably thought I ran away from the demonstration. The names were in the newspaper of all the people who were released from prison. Not my name. They were all released together in the same place, the journalists were there with questions, the photographers took pictures of the reunited families. I was thrown out on the road, like this." She pointed to her arm and face. "Two days before the formal release. No one even knows I was in jail."

I suggested that when she was feeling better, she'd want to tell the others, file a report, the usual. Though she tried not to sound angry, Lucia did present me a steely edge. "No one needs to know."

"Not for their sake, for yours, to get it off your chest." I tried to stop there, but after another glance at Lucia's face, seeing her wince as she reached for a glass of water, the words rushed out. "It's bigger than you or what I think or Hector's worries. The police beat you, they broke your arm, and threw you out on the road. Someone has to know. You can't stay quiet, not now, not after all the protests. Why were you dumped on the road? Why, if they planned to release you, why this way?"

"You don't understand. If I file a complaint, they'll ignore me or kill me or torture Hector, maybe even hurt Rebecca. Now, they don't know me, I'm just a body hauled off and dumped. I'm safe."

Maybe it was my anger, maybe it was affection for Hector and Lucia, maybe it's my character, though now writing it here, I'm surprised and relieved to report I had the nerve to ask Lucia, "What happened?"

"I don't know how to tell."

"Start at the beginning." I held my breath.

She laughed, sounding more like Hector in her laughter than

in her speech. "I'd rather start about six months from now."

I said nothing, only nodded assent. I felt much the same. Six months from now, back home, even the Christmas season would be over and the new year begun. By then, the governor of Oaxaca might have left office (as an act of generosity to the public) and the real, just, and decent people would be leading the State to a new and hope-filled future. Dreams.

"I was only in that prison for one night, but it was the worst night of my life. I think the other woman there with me might be dead by now."

"Dead? Do the police know?"

"They're the ones who killed her."

"Maybe an international group, witnesses?"

"They can't get into the prisons. They might help, but it takes time. There's no time when you're there. You don't have any time to wait. Things happen very fast and you can't stop them. You know if you try to stop them, it will be worse. Do you understand me?"

"They could have killed you, too." I didn't know if this was a question or a statement.

"She was an old woman, maybe seventy or eighty. An old woman who had worked too hard all her life, maybe she was only sixty. She was very small and thin, there was almost nothing to her and . . . you don't want to hear this."

My eyes opened wider. Only crazy people *want* to hear these stories, yet once they exist, once they come to life, they are stories that have to be told. And the telling requires at least one listener.

Besides, if this old woman had died, someone ought to be held responsible. Something had to be done. I could feel my Anglo spirit, such as it was, that outrage of entitlement, coming to life.

Equal rights, justice—we all know the words. People are tortured, disappeared, murdered, and no one is held responsible. There is no justice. The dead are faceless and the killers are faceless, all treated like outdated machinery left to rust in an abandoned field on the edge of town. But for family and friends of the disappeared, the tortured, the slaughtered, there is present-day, profound grief.

Each body had a mother and a father. Many of the bodies had sisters and brothers, spouses and lovers, aunts and uncles, all relations, good friends, close friends, acquaintances, a cat or a goat or a beloved bird. One corpse may have been a living human loved and missed by a fistful of yellow feathers shaped into a canary. Maybe only one bird stopped singing.

The archeologists in the future will have to dig hundreds of feet down to find any remnants of our world that lived by war. And they won't be able to understand the many twisted bodies, each with a hole in the back of the head. When one brilliant scholar theorizes that in ancient times the people killed one another en masse, the rest will drive him from the Academy. Absurd, crazy, preposterous, unscientific.

"You don't want to hear this, do you?" Lucia pulled me back.

"No, I don't want to hear, but I want you to tell me." That was as close to the truth of it as I could get.

I knew Lucia's anger was not at me, though her expression said something like, "You asked for it." She began in a wild rush of words, as if gaining momentum to make it through to the end of her story At times I had to ask her to repeat or to slow down because I hadn't quite understood the Spanish. Otherwise, as we sat there together, I remained listening, hearing, doing the thing I said I didn't want to do.

"I was in the front line at the march, part of a group of women who were leading. Behind us, the men carried a helicopter made of paper and wire with an effigy of the governor about to jump. Then beyond them, thousands, tens of thousands of people. The women wanted to be in front because we were concerned that the men would become violent. We wanted to send a clear message of peace. There is so much anger toward *El Tirano,* we knew the march could go in another direction, especially with the recent failure of efforts to negotiate and with the threat of police intervention. No support is coming from the federal government. Since Fox is about to leave office, he doesn't care. The politics are complicated and everyone will tell you a different story, but with young men on the front line facing other young men, a violent confrontation was possible. So, two hundred of us women, all dressed in our traditional clothes, led the march into the zócalo. I never told Hector this plan. I told him I would be safe in the middle of such a big crowd."

"Hector and I saw the march. We sat there, eating, talking about dance while you were . . ." As dramatic as the crowd had been, I have to admit I had been more absorbed in Hector's personal story. After meeting Angela, her images had replaced the remnants of my own: all those people on the other side of the glass, walking, chanting—they could have been a double row of willow trees whipped into action by a strong wind.

"Don't worry, it's not a problem. Hector couldn't have helped. All along the route of the march, there were no police, no militia, just a helicopter flying above us. They could have shot us with guns or maybe worse, with their cameras. That was enough of a threat. Still our spirits were very strong, so many people marching together. Do you know what this feels like?"

"I marched once in Washington DC against the Vietnam War, but I was young and was there to be with my friends. I have a fear of crowds."

"We were afraid too. All of us were afraid. You have to be, but the feeling of so many people fighting for change, fighting peacefully—our hearts were full. I had no malice, truly, not even toward the governor. It may sound strange, but at least our women's collective had studied together the need for a tranquil heart if we were to make change without violence. Some of the women carried bouquets of flowers to remind us of the traditional way the gods speak. Sometimes we chanted, sometimes we sang for the hope of a better future. And we walked toward the zócalo. People had bussed in from all over the state of Oaxaca, some, too, from other parts of Mexico. Some people walked from several miles on the highway, others joined us closer in. I felt like I was the river, a part of the river, but also the whole river. You know, we were all part of this river, and we traveled together. The enemy was also with us.

"This is the first time I've talked about it since the march. I thought they had taken away even my ecstasy. As we approached the zócalo, we heard sirens and saw that truckloads of militia had been brought in from the other direction. The zócalo was surrounded by police, and at all the corners there were water cannons mounted on trucks. I felt the hand of my friend next to me searching for my hand, and then on the other side, a woman I hardly knew, her hand was in mine. Down the whole front line, we all held hands tightly. We didn't expect this force to meet us. The hands I held were sweaty from heat and fear.

"As planned, the young women with the bouquets walked up to the police standing guard and handed them the flowers. The men held the flowers for a few beautiful, calm seconds, then what did they do? The police, now turned into awkward boys, looked at one another and down at the flowers and at the girls. Before we even had a chance to see, the water cannons blasted into the crowd and everyone began swarming. Some of the young men tore up the cobbled streets to get rocks, and they threw bottles at the police. The women tried to stay together. The older men tried to stop the stone throwers. We didn't even know who they were. In the chaos, it was impossible to stop them.

"Then I felt the stick hit me here on my face, then on my back. A strong arm pulled at my shoulder, and someone else handcuffed me. I didn't know where I was or who I was. I think I fainted in the police truck. We were crowded in, many of us wounded, and several people had collapsed. I felt it would be better to die and kept my eyes closed, though I couldn't close my ears; I wasn't the only one in pain, but I could do nothing to help. My heart had been full of courage, and then it was empty."

I wanted to tell Lucia our hearts can fill again even when we've been beaten down. Instead I sat there nauseated by a pure and solemn disgust for the whole human race. I'm sorry, but I'm sure you would have felt the same. How could anyone have hurt this woman?

"I have no idea how long I was in the truck. When we got to the prison, I was taken away from the rest and not even registered there. Maybe, I thought, they realized what a mistake they were making and were turning around to take the wounded to the hospital. The blood was dried on my face, but my eye was swollen shut and the waves of pain in my shoulder wouldn't stop. Of course they would take care of me. There had been a mistake. I remember trying to smile at the prison guard, imagining that he was a good guard, a guardian, that this would all be over soon, that he would personally escort me to the hospital. I believe I had gone insane.

"I was taken into a cell with one other woman, an old woman. They took off the handcuffs, but my shoulder was so torn and swollen, I could barely move it. The old woman smiled at me from her ragged blanket on the floor. I tried to speak to her. Her only language was Mazatec. I understand a dialect of Zapotec, but Mazatec is a different language. We did our best with sign language and her few words of Spanish. She pointed to my face, shook her head, and tears came down her face. She touched my shoulder very gently—maybe she was the guardian angel I had imagined. Later, when they finally brought water, she helped to wash my wounds. At times she chanted a prayer under her breath. If she hadn't been there, I'm sure I would not have survived. She kept us both alive with her prayers.

"There was a small window high up so I could see when night had come. I still hadn't been registered at the prison. Except for the water and a couple tortillas, we had been brought nothing and seen no one. I stopped imagining they knew they had made a mistake. I was haunted by thoughts of the disappeared, so many who go to prison and no one ever knows. I pictured Hector crazy with worry, but I could do nothing. I could think nothing but the worst. Mostly the Mazatec prayers were welcome, other times they made me feel crazier, but when the window space turned black, the old woman curled up and went to sleep. I tried to sleep, but the pain was too much. All that kept me breathing was the thought that Hector needed me, that he had lost his father so young and that he could not lose his mother. That's all, only Hector.

"He's not back, is he?" Lucia almost jumped at the thought he might have heard her.

"No, not yet, after the farmacia, he was going to visit Macario."

"El curandero?"

"Yes."

"What do you think of him?"

"I don't know him, we haven't met. He's been very good for Hector, hasn't he?"

"In some ways," she said.

"Lucia, they left you and the old woman alone there in the cell and no one came?"

"People came. In the middle of the night. I heard men talking outside the door. 'Is she in this one?' 'No, that one.' 'But the old woman is in there.' 'Yes, she's in with the old woman.' 'Why did you put her in with the old woman? I told you to put her alone.' Then, three men came in. I could barely see them, only from a flash of light from the hallway, one man maybe forty, the others were boys, younger than Hector. One of the boys was simple and the boss called him Stupid. The older man grabbed me, and I screamed out from the pain in my shoulder. 'Tie her mouth and blindfold her,' he said. 'You, Stupid, you fuck the old lady.' He said he didn't want to. 'Shut up and fuck her. You, Darling' (he called the other boy Darling), 'you wait 'til Stupid is done.' He kept talking like that to the two boys, even when he was grunting and coming inside of me."

I closed my eyes. I wanted the image of Lucia's rape to disappear.

"So you see?" she said to me.

"I'm afraid I do." I was crying by then.

"Fucking bastards," she said. "How can they do this?" Lucia was crying too, but it was harsh, as if she were crying ice drops.

I told her I didn't know, but I did know it had nothing to do with sex. It's a kind of war that men win for a few minutes. In the end, they lose everything.

"And so do the women." Lucia's one furious eye shone brighter than before. "But what would you know?" She was vindictive, though it was hardly personal.

I suppose, sitting there as I was in my tidy USA clothes, a well-preserved white woman, it was reasonable to think I had never been hurt. Reasonable, maybe, but naïve. "I was raped when I was sixteen. I wasn't brutalized, physically; I wasn't in prison. It's true, I don't know your experience, only my own. Lucia, at least half the women I've known have been raped, including several girls in my own family. What happened to you is horrific. It's so frightening, so terrible. Those men should be murdered."

"When they raped the old woman, at first she cried out. Her breathing was very strange, then I heard nothing. I pretended she was whispering her prayers, but I was almost sure they had killed her. They left me on the floor with the gag in my mouth, then tied my legs before they left. Sometime later, minutes or hours, I have no idea, a woman guard came in. She untied me.

"When she took off the blindfold, I saw that my cellmate was gone. 'Where is the old woman?' I asked. 'They released her.' I tried to tell the guard what had happened, but she didn't listen. It didn't matter to her. She was a woman, but she didn't care. She was just like the men.

"'What do you expect, a beauty like you?' the guard said to me. 'And a beauty like the old woman, why her?' I yelled, but my throat was too sore to make much noise. 'They did nothing to her, she was gone from the cell before they came in.' I pointed to where the old woman had been sleeping. 'She was here, right there.'

"Then the guard slapped me and held my shoulders. 'Look at me,' she said. '*La vieja* was not here. She was released last night. Her family came for her.' The guard's parting words were 'Forget everything.'

"It was still dark when the men came. Someone pressed a gun into my ribs, while another man pulled my arms back and tied my hands together. I cried out from the pain. He told me if I made another sound, he'd shoot me. They blindfolded me, then led me through a building, out several doors, and into the backseat of a car. We drove far away from the prison. No one spoke. The roads were rough and winding. Without use of my hands to brace myself, I was thrown from one side of the car to the other.

"I was certain my life had come to an end, that I'd be found days from then. Rotting on the road.

"Finally, one of them said, 'Stop there.' Those were the only words spoken on the entire drive.

"I was pulled out of the car and pushed to the side of the road in the middle of nowhere. One of the men untied my hands. I heard him run back to the car. I rushed to pull off the blindfold, to see the men, to see the car, just to see! I don't know why they didn't kill me. No one knew I was there, no one knows I've come back, no one knows what happened to me. The old woman was released, released where? The woman guard saw nothing, she says nothing happened, the only guards' names I heard were Stupid and Darling. Hector must have told you the rest, how he picked me up. I don't know if my arm will ever be right again.

"I know you didn't want to hear what happened, but that's it, as much of it as I can tell you."

By the time she got to the end, I felt as shaky as I had been when Hector drove me to the house. Only now I couldn't blame it on rutted roads. When it dawned on me that Lucia probably had not told the doctor about the rape, I pleaded with her to get help right away. Maybe I was making up for a time years ago when I had no one to tell, when I wouldn't tell, when I was ashamed, but I was determined that Lucia would get help. After much discussion, she finally agreed that she would get more care. Then she closed her eyes in sleep.

I decided to wait in the kitchen until Hector came back. Alone at the table, I let myself cry wholeheartedly. A kind of relief came to me because I had been able at least to do for someone else what I had been unable to do for myself. They say you can't help other people until you've repaired yourself, but it isn't true. If it were, the human condition would be far worse than it is and we'd have to rename even the clear blue sky "despair."

Hector returned an hour later with a bag from the farmacia and the newspaper. The headline story featured a woman, seventy-five years old, found dead on the road outside the city. There was one photograph of her supplied by the family and one taken in the morgue. She was identified as the grandmother of one of the teachers who was striking in a village northeast of Oaxaca. Her grandson said she had disappeared ten days earlier. He said his grandmother was taken, instead of him, to hurt the family all the more, to keep him from organizing. The police said she was caught stealing a shirt. A human rights group demanded an autopsy. There were signs that she had been violated sexually.

"Don't show this to your mother. Not now," I said to Hector.

"Don't show me what?" Lucia had gotten out of bed and was heading into the kitchen.

Abashed and reluctant, I handed her the paper. For a few seconds I managed to hope this was a different old woman, not that it would make the news itself any less grim.

"Mi vieja." Lucia went back to her room with the paper. She was sobbing now in a way that sounded more like screaming.

I stood up to go to Lucia but felt Hector was owed an explanation. "Your mother shared a cell with la vieja in the prison. Later, the woman was gone. According to the guard she had been released. That old woman was very kind to your mother, maybe saved her life with Mazatec prayers."

"Mama told you? About prison?"

"Yes, she told me."

NEVER TELL A MAN

One leaves home for a paradise, but when paradise turns tough as an old shoe, it gets called *real*. After my meeting with Lucia, my life in Oaxaca became real. Her prison story was the focus for all I did not want to know about my particular paradise. As others who have been sent from Paradise, I had lost innocence, and in its place, I was trying to be happy with experience.

A few days after our talk, I called Lucia. She had been steadily on my mind since our meeting; I was anxious to see her. Hector answered. He was quiet on the question of how his mother was feeling. Maybe she was in the room, but he did invite me to visit.

Classes had resumed at the university. Hector suggested once again I go with him to the dance class. He had told Macario about me, God knows what, and Macario had requested that I come to class. Seems I had appeared in one of his dreams or visions, but I didn't ask any more. I wasn't interested in discovering my totem insect, which, considering my current condition, was most likely a pill bug, curled inside itself and gray. I wasn't feeling very positive about men in general. I suppose we all have good and bad times with the opposite gender. The days after hearing Lucia's story were among the worst of my bad days and were accompanied by nightmares calculated to magnify the discomfort. In one, a man chased me through a house with uncountable doors and very high ceilings. It had a complex dreamscape design, filled with staircases, too steep and too narrow. I didn't know if I was going up or down or where the man was in relation to me. I just knew I had to get away. Eventually I woke up and turned on the light. There was an empty room, filled with nothing more than heartbeats, terror, and the bed I was sleeping in.

I told Hector I'd love to visit, but I wasn't sure I had the time to go to the dance class. He said to come soon, he'd be leaving for class in a couple hours.

"Don't be afraid. Macario said you can watch if you don't want to dance, but he wants to meet you."

I tend to have a soft spot for anyone who *wants* to meet me, even philandering curanderos.

"I think he wants to ask you about Lydia, too."

So much for being wanted.

After I hung up the phone, I cried for a full five minutes. I wanted to be home in my familiar exercise classes with reliable women instructors, in my own car on streets I can almost drive blind, in a culture I understood, even if it baffled me. I wanted to have a long talk with a trusted friend. The dams were overflowing, the way they do in me sometimes. Hector and Lucia had become my friends. Now the feelings one has for friends were coming in fast and hard. Yet they were friends I would soon have to leave and friends I may never be able to trust with my life, though they had entrusted me with theirs. Was I put on earth only to listen and to record? Did I have nothing to confide in them? More than once in the next half-hour I picked up the phone to tell Hector I was sick, then slammed it back down. I couldn't let anxiety get the best of me. Besides, it was a lie. I felt fine.

Even though the bus stopped near their house, I did pamper myself by taking a cab to Hector's. The cab driver had a hole in his forehead. You might call it a deep indentation. When I asked how the traffic was flowing, he gave the usual response: not to worry, no problem, he knew the best routes. Then he followed with a typical question: Was this my first time in Oaxaca, did I like it? Yes, very much, my favorite place.

Still he wanted to know why I was staying so long in Oaxaca. "Don't you miss your family?"

"It gives me time to write stories."

We were quiet through the next traffic jam, then he got chatty and told me about the indentation. "When I was young, I used to get drunk all the time and get in fights. One night I got into a fistfight with a guy who was really strong. He punched me square in the forehead so hard that I actually died. I saw heaven! All my ancestors were waiting for me, but then I heard the voices of my living family. They pulled me back to earth.

"I died and came back—and that was my last fight." His eyes glistened as he spoke. Backlit by the late afternoon sun, he appeared as an angel surrounded in light. "My last drink, too." We both laughed as he took a right turn away from the sun and landed back on earth.

Angel or not, he did know his way around the blockades, so despite all my weepy procrastinating at home, I was delivered to Hector's well before he had to leave for class.

Lucia opened the door for me. Her arm was still in the sling. My hello hug was also one-armed, very light, to her good side. She accepted it, along with a kiss into the air by her cheek. Much of the swelling was down in her face, and the bruises had faded a little from deep purple to purplish green. I could see more of her now, her expression and her beauty. Lucia was unnaturally calm, almost floaty. She told me Hector would be ready soon and offered me fruit water, which I declined on grounds that I had better not, before dancing. Dancing? Was I still thinking of it?

"I talked to the doctor. He came here. I told him more. He gave me medicine. For my nerves." She sounded more beaten down than she had when we first talked. "It helps me to sleep and to forget." The doctor had told her again that she was lucky to be alive. "He's wrong about my luck. I'm not alive. I'm dead. But," she added, "you can't tell your patient she's lucky to be dead, can you?"

"You won't stay feeling dead, you'll come back when you're ready."

She began to laugh almost hysterically. "Ready for what? For more of this?" Now in both of her eyes I could feel the blaze; it burned to ash my wooden attempt at solace. Then she began to cry and a minute later yelled at Hector to get himself into the kitchen. I was floored by the abrupt changes of mood.

He rushed in. "It's all right, Mama," was all he could say, as he patted her arm. "It's okay."

She pulled away from him. Before she shut the door to her own room, Lucia said to both of us, "I'm a dead woman. They killed me." Her face had turned to stone.

Hector found his mother's pills on the kitchen counter and brought them to her. She had become quiet and evidently took the medicine without argument.

As Hector and I were about to leave for his class, she called out again. "Open my door."

"She can't stand to have the doors shut, but she closes them herself. She's not normal anymore," Hector said. He was shaking his head as if to ward off the reality.

I went to open her door, and now she was smiling at me. It was like the welcome she had given me when we first met, days before. "I don't know what's wrong with me. I'm sorry. I know you want to help."

I suggested she get in touch with other women who were on the front line with her, but she didn't want any of them near her house. She didn't want to see them or talk to them, even though only a few days earlier she had told me how ecstatic it was to be part of this peoples' movement. I was shocked by the change in her. She let me know I didn't understand what was going on in Oaxaca. It would be best if I didn't understand. It was dangerous. She was convinced the police were watching the house, though she had never given her full name or address to anyone in the prison. She thought the phone was tapped. Mostly, Lucia was very worried they might take Hector from her. "He hates politics. They don't care. They'd do it to torture me more."

Even though Hector was in the kitchen waiting to leave

for the class, she asked me to sit down. Now, again, there was a hazy becalmed atmosphere around her. Her whisper was almost disembodied, as if channeled by a spirit being, but her question hit me with the force of a heavy hammer. "When you were raped, so young, how did you ever live again?"

The rape was over forty years past. I had tossed the experience into the heap of unwanted and useless, though I hadn't gotten beyond the sorting to the actual removal. It was clear Lucia wanted to talk more—this was one of the rare times she had asked me anything so personal, so direct.

"Do you mind if I stay here with you? I don't need to meet Macario. To tell you the truth, I'm too old for a dance class." I was relieved to have a real excuse.

Hector was ruffled at being told I had changed my mind, but after looking for a few moments at his mother and me, he seemed to realize it was best to leave us alone. We both wished him a good class, but I didn't say a final good-bye, as I had decided I would stay until he returned. As far as I could tell, Lucia did not want to be left alone.

"Maybe best you keep away from Macario," she said to me after Hector had left.

"I thought he's like a father to Hector."

"He wouldn't be like a father to you."

I shrugged. I hadn't wanted to be alone with any man for several days. The last agreeable sensation of that nature was lunch with her son, Hector. Though I have to say, the cab driver who returned from the dead was also a kind man, made sweeter by his glimpse of heaven. In any case, I felt irritable at the mere mention of Macario. I was sick of the steady pressure to meet him and had lingering suspicions from the conversation with Lydia on my last flight from Oaxaca.

"I don't remember feeling dead. I don't remember feeling anything at all except guilty, as if I had done something more wrong than any wrong I had ever done."

"What did you do wrong?"

"I don't know. I was a kid, Lucia, I don't even remember." That wasn't the truth. Over the past few days I had begun to remember all of it, in fact had searched my memory for anything more I could remember, any shred of anything sensible I did that night. I could only remember one thing. "I didn't resist. I didn't fight him. I should have fought him off, screamed and kicked and bitten him, but I was afraid I would be hurt."

"You're right. He could have killed you."

"I asked him to."

"I don't understand."

"I asked him to kill me. I didn't want to live. He started to strangle me. When I felt his hands around my throat, I pushed him away. I changed my mind in two seconds. You know how it is—sometimes a taste is enough."

"You were lucky. He could have done it."

"*Lucky,* like you were lucky. Like women everywhere, every country, every age, in times of war, and in times of peace. Some women are so damaged they can never—"

"I never will," she said. "They did kill the other woman. If I had been old, it would have killed me, too."

As we talked about the condition of women, I beseeched her again to get help, not to stay alone in the house taking tranquilizers for the next six months. She was frozen, terrified to leave home, afraid they would find her, they would see her on the streets, they would drive by in a white van and throw her inside, take her back to prison. I eventually realized that my suggestions and well wishes were not making a dent in her acute anxiety. It wasn't a question of mere consolation. We both lapsed into silence. In that space, I searched my own experience for an answer to Lucia's question: How did you ever live again?

After I was raped, I was afraid the police would find me. The man took me back to the party we had both attended. I'm lying. He was at a different party, a different race. (We used to be able to say what race. Now it's no longer possible, as if it condemns the whole race. Instead we condemn the whole gender.) He was at a party in the other apartment on that floor. He was probably ten years older than my sixteen. At my party, there were a bunch of rich prep school kids, out of school for summer, drinking, smoking, looking for meaning in a skewed way.

I had no idea where I was, somewhere in a ramshackle part of Boston. The man had no name, not even then, or did he have a name? What he had, he said, was a store. He said he owned a store, and he wanted to show it to me. Sure, why not? Mom had taught me to treat people of all races as equal. Besides, the boy, the smart boy destined for success, was ignoring me, and I was drunk. I was stupid and young.

I know it sounds strange, almost romantic, but I was going to have my own store that summer. I wanted to see his: how had he arranged things, what was he selling, how had he decorated? My friends and I were selling handmade jewelry, clothing, and imports from Mexico. I had gone with my mother to her friend's warehouse to choose the things to sell.

I found a little storefront to rent, cheap. It was in a tourist town on the Cape. I was telling him about my store, then (he was trying to make conversation) he said, "I have a store. Let me show you my store." We had been sitting at the top of the steep stairs that led to both apartments, to both parties. He had his arm around my shoulder in a friendly way. We walked down the stairs. There was a railing on the left side, a wall on the right side. At the bottom of the staircase, in front of the door, he pushed me against the wall and kissed me, too hard. Then we got on a bus. I didn't know where I was, and I didn't know where I was going. I was sad because the other boy didn't like me, and I was drinking, and here was this guy holding me and telling me he had a store. I was young and stupid. We sat in the bus, and I remember the night was warm, my dress was sleeveless, and the lights outside were holes in the darkness. There was no light. We traveled together on the bus in the dark night through the dark lights of the night. I don't remember getting out of the bus.

There was a cross on the door. The door was black with a white wooden cross on it and even though I'm not a Christian, I felt relieved because he was a good fellow with a cross on the door. There were no signs at the store, nothing tempting in the store windows. In fact, there were no windows or if there were, they had been boarded up. And in the bus, I had noticed he was different. If I said don't do this or don't do that, it didn't matter to him, he'd do it anyway. He was very muscular. I began to notice I might be in trouble, but when I saw the cross on the door I was relieved, even though there was no store sign, no windows. Maybe it was a Christian meeting place, a fellowship hall, I thought.

When he opened the door to show me his store, I saw it was

an empty room. There was nothing inside, except on the floor in the exact center of the room, there was one mattress, narrow and nearly flat. I wasn't relieved anymore. I wanted to go home. I didn't like him. He had lied to me about his store, and he was pushing me too hard. I was afraid, but I didn't know how to feel afraid.

"He could have killed me, but I was too scared to feel afraid of dying."

"When they raped me, by then, I was too dead to feel afraid," said Lucia.

"I was too young to feel dead and too scared to feel afraid. I didn't know what people can do. I didn't know that what I want or don't want isn't very important to some people."

"I was crazy, too. I thought the guards knew they made a mistake. I thought they would help me."

"It's normal, isn't it, to expect goodness?" My question hung in the air like a bare light bulb swinging from a plain brown cord.

When he went to the back of the room—maybe there was a bathroom—I ran to the front door and tried to get out, but it was locked. I couldn't undo the latches. They were complicated city bolts. When he came out, he said "You're not leaving yet," then pulled me down to the floor. The floor was dirty and so was the mattress. Everything was dirty except my dress that I had put on clean for the party. The dress had flowers on it, pretty and bright in oranges and pinks. I had been happy because school was out and it was summer. My friends and I were going to open the store the next week. I had chosen the merchandise and my mother was teaching me how to keep the accounts. It was such a pretty dress and summer was beginning.

Maybe this man liked me; maybe he wanted to be with me, I thought. The boy I liked didn't want me. My parents were away that weekend and left me home in the suburbs with a friend, we'd be fine. She had a car, we were practically grown up . . . sixteen . . . they could leave us alone at the house. My friend had heard about a party in Boston, let's go, the boys we like will be there. This man wanted me. He didn't want me to leave. He wanted me to stay there with him and that's all. I did what he wanted me to do. He wanted me to get excited so I did. It was a show. Then I asked him to kill me. But he didn't. He didn't do anything I wanted him to do. I did everything he wanted me to do. I was chicken. I didn't want to get hurt. I was young.

I don't know why he took me back to the party. He could have left me there on the street. Something about him, aside from being a rapist, was very strange. He wanted me to like him.

"That guy tried to rape me into liking him. I did what he wanted. I made it look like I liked him. Years later I thought he must have been a very lonely person who didn't know how to have real love."

"*Pobrecito*." Lucia's look of disgust made it hard to continue talking.

"Maybe that was when I returned to life."

"When?"

"When I thought of him as unable to love."

"How could you care?"

"I wanted to live. I cared for my own sake, not for his."

The bus back was empty, except for us. When we got to the stop, he didn't get off the bus. He pointed out the door of the building to me. It was unlocked. I walked up the stairs alone, slowly, holding onto the rail. My friend had left the party, left with the car and with the boy she liked. He liked her, too, so they had left, I guessed. I had no idea. Most of the party was gone or asleep by the time I returned. One boy I had never seen before was there, sitting on the couch. I told him I didn't know where my friend was. I tried to describe her, but he was too drunk or too tired, he couldn't remember her. I had to get home, but I didn't know how. I didn't even know where I was.

"Something strange happened. When I got back to where I thought my friend was, I told a boy there that I had been raped."

"Never tell a man."

"Sometimes you have to. There's no one else. You told the doctor, and he helped you."

"He told me I was lucky. You should never tell a man."

"They're not all the same. Anyway, he was a boy."

"So what did he do?"

"He tried to kiss me. He must have thought I was easy."

"See?"

"I told him to leave me alone. He was a regular kid who could be pushed away. I found the telephone. My friend drove all the way back into Boston to pick me up, then we went to my house in the suburbs. My parents' house was big, clean, always perfectly clean. My mother took good care of everything: house, clothes, food."

I had to get up three hours later to go to my brother's college graduation in another state. I don't know how I got there. All I remember was wearing a new dress, blue and white checks. It was cut low. I had bruises all over my neck and chest, some on my arms. When my mother saw me, she asked what I had done the night before. I told her, "I went to a party." She smiled. She was glad I had friends and went to parties. She used to worry because I was shy. Maybe my long hair covered the bruises; maybe she didn't see them.

"What did your mother do, when you told her?"

"I didn't tell her. I didn't even consider telling her. I had done something so wrong, I couldn't tell my mother."

"I'd tell my mother, if she were alive."

"It's different. Politics. It's real. You couldn't help it. You were tied up. This was a party. A bad party. I went with him. I didn't fight him."

"Didn't you tell a friend?"

"After his graduation, I drove home alone with my brother. I told him."

"Never tell a man."

"Come on, Lucia, my brother was barely a man, not even twenty-two years old. Hector's age. He told me I needed help. I cried. I was confused. My brother didn't know what to do."

"They don't know," Lucia said.

"You haven't told Hector, then?"

"No, I'll never tell my son. He wouldn't understand. He'd go crazy."

"What's there to understand? None of it makes sense."

"He'd hate me for it."

"You couldn't have stopped it. It wasn't your fault. You had no choice."

"If I had asked, they would've killed me. I should have asked."

"You were gagged."

I don't know why Lucia and I smiled at one another. Maybe we had gone to the depths together and were ready to come up for air. Maybe it was the wretched, stupid fact of it: she couldn't ask to be killed because she was gagged. Because she was gagged, maybe it saved her life. Maybe they wouldn't have killed her, even if she had asked.

Lucia's smile quickly faded. "They did kill me."

I had no answer. One day I'd see Lucia and she'd be better—changed, but better. She would come back to life. I didn't know how. Maybe, like my taxi driver, a living family would pull her from hell back into the ordinary, the beautiful world.

Hector returned from school early. Women had taken over the radio and the TV stations. Only women, all women. Classes were canceled. The police were out preparing to storm the stations. Hector had barely made it back to the house and was in no mood for anything. "All I want to do is get back to my classes. I'm sick of all this shit."

"I'm going," she said. "I have to help them." Lucia tried to get out of bed. Hector and I were alarmed and both began to speak at the same time with our different forms of "No, for God's sake."

Fortunately, whatever the doctor had given Lucia was making her dizzy, and though she seemed one second to be ready to take action, a minute later, she was quiet, settled back in bed.

"I can't go. The hell with them," she said.

I felt pretty much the same way. Hector, also, nodded in agreement.

Re-visiting the night I was raped had drained me far more than I'd expected. I wanted to get back to my place, e-mail a friend, and have a beer or two, alone. I felt overexposed.

As I reached for my purse in preparation for leave-taking, Hector brought up the now tired subject of el curandero. "I saw Macario tonight. We all left school together. He wants to see you. I told him we'd call him when I got back, make a time to meet."

"Hector, I don't have the time or patience right now, maybe next time I come to Oaxaca in the winter. He can write to Lydia if he wants to know how she is. He doesn't need me for that. I'm not up for magic and healing."

"Macario saved my life. He's a great man. He doesn't want to see you about Lydia, you know that."

I knew nothing but had no energy to argue. "Call him," I said. "I can meet him tomorrow."

Lucia motioned me back to her. "You watch out." I thought she winked. "He's a very handsome man."

I was completely undone by this comment from Lucia who had been warning me against men, including Macario, for the previous two hours.

"What is it I should watch out for?" I asked her in all honesty.

She was finished with the conversation. Her eyes closed and her breathing grew steady. As Lucia moved farther away from the waking wars and closer to the one, whole connected world of deep sleep, she looked happier than I had seen her. When Hector returned from making the call, I put a finger to my lips to keep him quiet. He smiled, seeing his mother asleep.

"You have an appointment with Macario tomorrow at eleven."

"An appointment? I don't want—"

"You can meet at his office."

"I thought you'd be there, too. We'd all go out for coffee. I don't need—"

"I can't leave my mother tomorrow. Here's the address."

Hector handed me Macario's business card, we exchanged a quick hasta luego, then I walked outside, glanced up at the moonlit sky, and raised my arm to hail the next passing taxi. I didn't feel like taking the bus.

SUSPICION

The morning was cool with clouds lingering low after a midnight rain. Because I had an hour or two before the sun would break through full force, I decided to take the two-mile walk to Macario's office and enjoy the morning. As I walked, I resolved to make the visit brief, then spend a few hours in the tourist haunts if, in this time of political protest, any could still be found. With only four more days in Oaxaca, I needed to purchase the promised gifts. During the next several blocks, my plans expanded to include getting myself a few essential mementos and dining at a favorite seafood restaurant. I relished the idea of one of the "old" Oaxaca days of unmitigated tourism.

The *flamboyan* trees were in full bloom; vermilion flowers nestled in the deep green foliage. Coral roses were all set to open, the scent of white jasmine lightened the air, the ruffled dark red hibiscus flopped from their branches, and deep yellow blossoms still spread wide on the *calaverita* trees. I ignored continual car honks, black bus exhaust, broken-up sidewalk, occasional blasts of music, bass thumps, and dog snarls from the rooftops.

No matter where you are, you have to choose your own walk.

About a half mile from Macario's office, my attention shifted to the wood smoke and sweet smell of corn emanating from a *tortilleria*. An old woman was approaching from the other direction. As she shifted her belongings, a cloth napkin, the kind used to carry tortillas, fell from her bag. She hadn't noticed. A few steps later when I arrived at the spot, I stooped over to pick it up for her. A streak of familiar sciatic pain raced up my leg and into my lower back.

La Señora gave me a fine, nearly toothless smile and nodded a thank you. For three seconds our eyes met—there was nothing old or rheumy or toothless about her eyes. They were as clear and fierce as a jaguar's. I continued on my way, assuming I would walk out the pain, but my lower back became more tense. By the time I arrived at Macario's office, all I wanted was to lie down. I decided I'd say hello, get in a taxi, and go back home.

The office was no longer at his house as Lydia had told me, but an address five blocks from a main thoroughfare. Maybe he had an office for beautiful young women separate from his office for the rest of us. When I walked in, he was standing in the reception area. No one else was in the office.

"Macario? I'm Carol, Hector's friend."

He gave me a warm smile and the usual kiss on the cheek, a pat on my upper arm. His touch was light, familiar. Though we had only just met, we were victims of closeness by hearsay. His eyes were nearly black, and when I looked into them, the room went out of focus. I took a step back, pitched my gaze through the window, and the world returned to normal.

To my green *gringa* eyes, Macario was a handsome man. Long black hair pulled back from his face—other than the hair, his features aroused images of my father as a young man: full lips, long, well-formed nose, a graying mustache, glasses. He seemed to be one of my family. My concerns about his integrity disappeared immediately. I felt embarrassed to have been so suspicious of him. He was a kind, well-intentioned man.

When Macario asked me in the ordinary polite way how I was doing, I told him, as a matter of fact, I was fine until about fifteen minutes ago when I reached down to pick up a tortilla cloth for an old woman and felt a return of sciatica. I was in pain, I told him, and though I had hoped to visit longer, now I wanted to get back home. His back seemed to twitch in response to my description.

"I can help you."

"I need to go home and rest. I'll be better."

"You can lie down here."

I would have objected, but nothing about him hinted at anything other than the gracious host-healer.

He showed me into his treatment room, suggested I take off my shoes and loosen my clothes. Once I was settled on the narrow table, he adjusted pillows for my knees and neck. He sat down on a stool next to me, and we began to talk. It wasn't the café encounter with Hector, our mutual friend in tow, that I had imagined. In truth, I felt more relaxed in this place where it was relatively quiet, cool, and dimly lit. Macario gave me his full attention. And I gave him mine. He told me about his family, his upbringing as the grandson of a curandera, and his training as a dancer. I had heard many of the stories before from Lydia and Hector, but without their emotional attachments, his life was more believable and much funnier. He often portrayed himself as the center stage clown in the midst of a roiling tragic drama. I talked to him about the stories I was writing, including the one about Lydia. As Hector had warned me, Macario wanted to hear more about her. I told him what Lydia had experienced in the temazcal, which surprised him, as "all life did." He was intensely curious about people and never claimed any magical power. He knew his good work came about through the grace of spirit, a spirit not within his control. He had no personal arrogance. I said nothing about Lydia's confused longing for him, only that I thought he had helped her.

"She liked you very much."

"Yes, yes, she's an interesting person." He raised his eyebrows but did not stroke his mustache. I was glad of that.

He asked nothing more about Lydia, just talked freely about his own life. It was easy to be with Macario. He was friendly and open, also smart and cultured—a city boy with country skill. Before long, he suggested a massage for my back and legs in order to relieve the pain, then maybe we could go out and have some coffee, if I felt like it.

It had been eons since I had spoken to a handsome man while reclining, and I found it entirely pleasant. Perhaps, also, he could locate the deeper source of my sciatic irritations. Though Macario never suggested anything other than help in the moment, I have to admit I was considering the possibility of a healing revelation.

Macario left the treatment room while I took my clothes off

and got under the sheet, face down in the hole, as he had directed. When he went out, he turned on some quiet music, and I did think it could be the start of a seduction, but then remembered the massage therapists in the States played similar sap.

As he began to massage me, we both stopped talking. To be without words was a relief. Something other than mere quiet ensued. It goes against my grain to say "submissive calm" but it was true. The relaxation had as much to do with my "giving up" as it did with his "giving to." Macario did not attack particular points of tightness, as I now remember it, though these memories are fogged by other later memories and by thoughts and dreams. His hands seemed to even out my pain, as if dispersing a mob of discomfort, thus allowing each individual to return to daily life.

Maybe he had "healing hands." Or maybe we were friends. Maybe, near him, the cells of my body aligned along an amiable magnetic pole. Maybe with the help of spirit his cells were also moving into a fine, clear line. The nearest name I had for the feeling was falling in love, but having relinquished the idea of romance, I now had no words in which to float this experience. I let my questions drift downstream. And once again became aware of my own good fortune at having met Macario and in this way, at his office. It was one of the few times in my life I didn't struggle for happiness. It was right there with me. Maybe happiness had been right there with me all along and I hadn't noticed. I hadn't even made the appointment myself. I only appeared. I only had to say I was in pain. I only had to agree to lie down on this table.

When Macario touched me, I didn't experience my body as a collection of parts, some tense, some not, some lovely, some ugly. I was one whole alive person, which it struck me even at that time, is exactly how a person is meant to be.

There was only one glitch in this experience of wholeness. At first the massage was pure relaxation. Maybe halfway in, I became conscious of strong sexual feelings and faster breathing. As I knew this was a "clinical" relationship, I struggled to control myself, to calm down. It didn't work.

"My heart's beating." It was the first thing I said since naked with Macario.

"You have a lot of energy."

I guessed he was agreeing. I still didn't want any words between us, not to mention, talking with one's head in a massage table hole is almost impossible. I thought he might have a magical way of stopping the feelings, a hidden handle that could turn off the tap. Slow down the heartbeat.

As he went on working, his body was pressed against me and I began to perceive Macario had an erection and was breathing heavily along with me, which I took to be a form of shamanic breath control, certainly not a personal response to a real woman. In the United States we believe healing can only occur in an impersonal environment. If he, the man, was sexually excited around me, the woman, then I would get up from the table as sore as I had been when I first lay down. My cultural training convinced me I was experiencing a new kind of healing, despite the fact that I was lounging naked and panting on a massage bed.

"Can you turn over now?"

I had lost track of time and space; yet I moved around easily and my lower back seemed to be pain-free. I wouldn't know until I started walking and sitting, but just then, as I turned, I had hope.

I opened my eyes and enjoyed the sights. Macario's face was

much more attractive than his floor. "My back's better," I said.

He nodded and began to focus on my neck, shoulders, and chest. As breasts were included, my body began breaking up into parts, but after several long strokes, the breasts once again joined my chest and my chest attached itself to the lower half. As I was being divided and reunited, I kept my eyes closed except for occasional peeks to note that Macario's eyes were wide and watching.

"I'm afraid to look," I said.

"Afraid of what?"

"You."

His eyes held open and dark, waiting to be filled with whatever meaning I poured into them. When his hand next reached mine, I curled my hand around his and held it. He didn't bring out the surveying tools to argue a professional boundary. We held hands.

The previous days had been so deep and discouraging: sitting with Lucia, hearing of the pain of men disconnected from love and the way disconnection can turn to brutality; talking about what the violence does to women, what it had done to Lucia, what it had done to me; and thinking of the countless people who had been severed from themselves through abuse and rape. It was all too much. I didn't believe I would ever in all my life want to hold another hand in mine.

I moved over to make room for Macario. "Sit here."

He sat next to me and brushed the hair off my forehead, the new bangs designed to mask the worry lines emanating from the bridge of my nose. Over and over he stroked the hair back as if he wanted to see deeper into me. I reached up to feel his shoulder. I wanted to soothe away his pain, though it was only in my imagination he had any pain to soothe away. I pulled him closer to me and we kissed. Our soft lips, one mouth, one body.

"We don't even know each other."

"Maybe we do."

After this interlude, Macario went back to the work of my body with his full attention, piecing the remaining fragments into one solid human. He left the room while I dressed, brushed the massage oil through my hair, and wiped away the black marks on my cheeks made from tears falling through mascara. My back and legs had returned to normal, as if I had never picked up the napkin for La Señora. When I took one last glance in the mirror, the old woman's face appeared in the room behind me. Her smile had fangs to match the jaguar eyes. I blinked, and she edged back into the surrounding air.

I asked what I owed him for the massage, but Macario wouldn't take any money.

"It's your work." And a question of my equilibrium, but I didn't say so.

He shook his head. "Let's have coffee."

We began walking. The café was a few blocks from his office, which gave me a chance to realize the sciatica was gone, but it had been replaced by something far worse: suspicion. I started fishing around, trying to find out if I was special to him or only another lonely client.

"Does it happen to you a lot?" I asked.

"Not a lot."

His answer felt abrupt and cold. I suddenly wanted to be done with this meeting laced with gratitude, arousal, phony familiarity, and uncertainty. It was awkward out in the big world with Macario. I didn't know him and from the sounds of his latest pronouncements, I never would. I was happy for Hector that he had a substitute father. It was clear Lydia had more or less misunderstood him, which, considering what I had just experienced, didn't seem completely crazy.

I put a heaping spoonful of sugar in the espresso and sipped at the light ring of foam. "Macario, I have to tell you something."

"It's okay, don't worry."

"Lydia. She told me you kissed her. It confused her. She thought you meant more by it."

"A kiss? I don't remember. I'm not there when I'm working. It's like a trance."

I lowered my voice. "Do you remember that we kissed?"

He laughed. "Yes, of course."

"You were alone, nearly naked in the temazcal with her."

"It's very hot in the temazcal. You have to sweat. A few times people have told me later they meet dead people. I don't know why this happens. Most times, it helps them."

"So you knew nothing about what was going on with her?"

"How could I know? It was her. I only held her."

"You do remember."

"No, nothing. A woman-spirit comes through me, but it's not me."

"How do you know when it is you?"

"Me is me." It was spoken like a true clown. We both laughed.

"Lydia was a little in love with you. She was confused between love and healing."

"They're the same."

I had a feeling I was getting nowhere. There was nowhere to

get, and nothing more than now appeared and nothing less. At moments, I wanted to shake Macario silly. Just say it, say you have sex with all your clients, tell me they all fall for you, tell me I'm simply another one in a long line of white female fools tickled pink by a dark man in trance. Then it dawned on me that the man was a manipulative genius. He didn't have to give the women alcohol or drugs to fog their recollections. Instead, he forgot! And called it feeling or spirit or trance. Macario had a market on the latest, greatest abuse of memory.

Expecting to see the face of a fraud, I looked at him again. I was met by honesty and clarity. This was the way the healing worked. He wasn't conniving. If his clients needed to make something else of it, he couldn't be held responsible, but then how did I fit in? I wasn't a paying client, we had touched as lovers, he did remember (so did I). Sitting here with him was happening in the moment, in real time, on this ordinary physical plane, and I couldn't shift it into another level of existence or regard it as part of my work of creating fictions.

Was this the healing game he was playing with me? To make love seem real in the real world in order to trick me into remembering love exists, that men are not only romancers and rapists? If so, the man was even more brilliant than I first imagined. He had used magic to make the world seem real. He was sitting with me in a café because I didn't need his trance state or a father or dead people. I needed a real cup of coffee. And he had to pay for it, the way men used to. But then what was he getting out of it? I couldn't answer.

Maybe he would always remember the kiss, but forget the cup of coffee, because the coffee was brought by spirit, the ordinary healed. Spirit knew I wouldn't truck with the extraordinary. Sitting there at the café, my convoluted romantic notions and dark suspicions were fast becoming a form of insanity. I slugged down the shot of espresso.

As we were saying good-bye, Macario asked me how long I would be in Oaxaca. Only four more days. Then, he suggested, why don't we meet again the next day. He'd show me a few galleries and we could have lunch together. I shuffled around in my mind for a quick escape but seemed to have forgotten the social steps. We were to meet at ten the next morning.

Hector called me that night. He wanted to know if I had met Macario. Yes. He sounded pleased. And your mother? Not quite so bad today, he said, maybe the drugs were working. And Macario, you had a good meeting? Yes, it was fine, he seemed familiar. I told you, Hector said, he wanted to meet you because he felt he knew you. I thought he only wanted to give massages to foreigners, I said. He gave you a massage? I hurt my back on the way there. He fixed it for me. It was quiet on Hector's side. I just wanted to know if you met, he said, and to say good-bye. Send my love to your mother and email me soon, tell me how you both are. And Hector, thank you for making the appointment. He's a good man. Yes, I said. And handsome? I answered with good-bye, *hasta luego*.

I went to sleep with a nervous tickle in my stomach, and I woke up with it as well. Walking to meet Macario, doubt weakened my ankles and knees. What if he had forgotten our meeting? What if I stood at the agreed-upon intersection and stood and stood, but he never arrived? What if I had imagined the time, the place, the man himself?

Nearly a block away, I could see Macario standing at the corner, waiting. I was truly happy to see him while at the same time tried to brace myself for his cool, comic, real-world demeanor. Despite a simmer of private ecstasy, to him I showed nothing more than the usual warmth of greeting. Other than an occasional fatherly hand or shoulder grab to keep me from getting run over by a car, we walked together as friends, argued about the purpose of art, discussed the dilemma of social justice, and compared the legal systems of our respective countries.

The galleries featured Oaxacan artists. Many of the paintings, beautifully executed and sometimes entrancing, were of a magic realist universe that I could best describe as a mix of Salvador Dali, Diego Rivera, and Marc Chagall. Though unlikely bedfellows, they were having an orgy in Oaxaca. At the last gallery, I was arrested by a painting of a jaguar-woman character climbing an adobe wall. The back of the cat and all four legs were visible, but the face, turned outward, was human.

"She looks like a woman in your office," I said. "I saw her after the massage, when I was getting dressed."

"You've been in Oaxaca too long."

"You mean there is no jaguar woman in your office?" I honestly didn't know if I was joking or not.

We were both smiling.

"If there is one, she wouldn't want me to see her," he said.

"Why?"

"Jaguars don't like to be seen. They're like you."

"Me?"

Turned out Macario wouldn't be able to have comida. He had booked a massage in the afternoon, but before I had time for a reaction, he suggested a short visit the following evening. He had business at my end of town, then could stop by. I told him I'd be home.

It was more than a nervous tickle that evening. Call it a throttle. Though I had purchased wine for the occasion, he didn't want any. We both sat at my table drinking glass after glass of cold water with lime. For a while we engaged in a mutual search for our connection—Frida and Diego in Detroit, Trotsky, Mexico City, my Russian heritage, artist friends of the family, then dancing, healing, writing, singing. The themes were all big and close to both our hearts, but they were well outside a personal, emotional connection. The conversation itself, the curiosity, drew us closer. We held hands again. And from there our talk took a different turn.

"How do dead people enter the temazcal?"

"It's not the temazcal they enter, it's the person. It could be anywhere."

"Then why all the hocus-pocus, the intense heat, the chanting, the claustrophobia?"

"It's what most people need to believe they can be something else. They need a strange place to find new possibilities. Not you."

"I have strange places: I sit in front of a computer and then there's Mexico. Are you telling me it's all in the imagination?"

"What do you think?"

After he asked, we began to kiss and before long we were in my bed, two naked people. It was true what he had said about me and the jaguar woman. I didn't want to be seen, but as it had been from the start, there was no good hiding place with Macario. As our arousal advanced, our conversation still continued. Perhaps I had gone into a trance in my own bed, but what I said next seemed to come from nowhere or elsewhere.

"I believe we hold other people inside of us, that we are like tombs. Each living person is the tomb for dead people, only inside of us they are alive . . . some of them."

"And the others?"

"We kill others inside of us, and they stay dead. Some people have only dead people living inside them. You can tell who they are because their eyes are empty. It's better to let the dead people leave your body. They kill you."

Macario was following every word. "What about the alive dead?"

"The ones you love stay alive in you and give you life, even though they are dead."

The conversation broke off while we loved, entwined, and grew closer to the source of our connection. So much was new and curious to me, I didn't know how to remain in my own body. He had less trouble and soon enough, was at rest again.

"It's possible," he said, "to kill people who are physically alive, to kill them inside of you, without a weapon."

"Can you do that?" I had a feeling he didn't mean it figuratively, and it gave me that out-of-focus sensation.

"I've seen it done. My teacher wanted to train me to do it. I left him."

"You left?"

"He taught me how to heal people. You have to get close to death many times in order to be able to this, but then he wanted to teach me the other side. He wanted me to do magic with him, to use it, to get things, to hurt people. At first he wasn't clear. He taught me little tricks, then later I could see. Everyone has a limit.

Everyone has a human face, even the great teachers. You have to know your own self or you can be led in the wrong direction."

"When you left him, was he angry? Did he try to hurt you?"

"No, no, nothing like that. He thinks I'll come back later and learn."

"You might?"

"No. I'm not going to hurt people."

Macario's goodness and normalcy were very appealing to me. Working in a realm fraught with discomforting mysticism, he was the funny straight man. My affection for him grew once again, as did his for me, and next thing I knew he was lying on top of me, using his arms to keep his full weight from pressing against me.

What about the women?

The women?

All the women you seduce.

I don't.

What about me?

You're a guide. I'm following you into a place I've never been.

Do you say that to all your women?

There's no All. Suspicion is the dead man living inside of you.

Macario knelt between my legs. His penis was like a bridge between us. We met there in the middle, exchanged feelings, then returned to our own shelters. The constant sway of his bridge created waves of excitement inside me. I could hear a brass band practicing in the village, burros bellowed, and a pack of dogs went howling down the street.

It's a suspicion born from the place where a man hurt you. He was born inside of you, when you were born and has grown with you. If you don't let him leave, you won't live. And I can't be there.

What does it matter? You're married.

Your man Suspicion has nothing to do with my marriage. How do you think it feels, to be inside of you with him there too?

As Macario seemed to be feeling just fine inside of me, I couldn't muster much sympathy. It's too bad you didn't stay with your teacher, he could have taught you how to kill the Other Man. I didn't know if this was my own voice or a dead person rising up from the tomb. Acid dripped from my tongue, and my teeth felt sharp.

I have learned how to kill pain. I can kill your lover Suspicion. It won't change your infidelity.

I can't share you with him. I need you.

After this, I couldn't talk. Every question from my old life rose up like fish jumping for bugs at sunset. How do you feel about me? Do I matter? How much? For how long? What are you thinking? Are you using me? Is it just sex? Do you love me? Do you love me more? The most? Then the fish disappeared into the pond, and the water turned from black to aquamarine. Waves lapped against the shore.

When I opened my eyes, I heard Macario whisper, "What a beautiful view." His black eyes seemed to be jumping inside my green ones. "Your eyes and your lips."

I returned the compliment. "You have the most beautiful face." The music of the neighborhood took over, and I moved with it into the fast, warm circles of a Latin dance, thus bringing our extended connection to its natural, physical end.

Macario lay next to me, cradling my head on his chest. As he talked about his children, his siblings, his parents, and grandparents, it was if we had known one another forever. I hardly spoke. Now his family stories are lost to me. His words were a river, and I was resting on the bank, in the warm shade of a willow tree, listening to the water rush. My words didn't matter either. Speech is sound, the voice of a lover is music, the music played by the river, the ripples of love running through all the land. The music pushed the clouds aside. The sun was still alive and willing to shine.

"Please, Macario, remember me." I was desperate, as if his memory alone could make all love real.

"Don't worry, Chica, I remember."

"Do you remember the dead man who lives inside me? The one you are jealous of?"

"I don't understand."

"You said you were jealous because a dead man named Suspicion lives inside of me."

"I'm sorry, I don't know. Did I say this?"

"I heard you say it. You said you'd kill him for me."

"Yes," he waved his arm around Zorro-style, "with my rubber sword."

"You said something else. You said I'm leading you to a place you've never been."

He looked at my face for a long time. I was happy during his examination as it gave me a chance to be alone with his face, a face that changed shape with frequency, keeping pace with the flight of my imagination.

"You have the eyes of my dance teacher," said Macario.

"The one in Paris?"

"She was from the States but lived most of her life in Mexico."

"Hector told me about one from Paris."

"We met there when I was twenty-two."

"Were you lovers?"

"I wanted, but she was older than me. She was afraid she'd scare me."

"How old was she?"

"Maybe fifty-eight, sixty."

"Maybe she was afraid you'd love her and leave her." I stretched my arm across his belly and took hold of his hand. "I wanted to be a dancer, but I didn't have the right body."

Looking puzzled, Macario glanced down at me. "It just takes work."

"I didn't know. I thought dance was something given."

"And your writing?"

"What about it?"

"Is it given?"

"Yes and no. You have to develop endurance."

"Many people tell me I should write my stories, but I'm not good at writing."

"I can help you." I had no idea how I could help a Spanish writer.

Only in that moment I was certain that one's native tongue made no difference. What matters in writing is to follow your own line through the maze, undaunted by the wrong turns and their dead ends.

There was a time a few years ago when my daughter had to wait for me, as we walked next to the Arno River. She had grown the strong legs of a twenty-year-old and I, at fifty, was moving too slowly for her. I remember the moment with a shock. Not so explosive as thunder and lightning arriving at the same instant, but a deeper shock, waving down and down into the mystery of life and death. "I can't keep up with you," I said, as she rushed into the streets of Florence.

Now lying in bed with Macario, another deep shock passed through me. I would no longer be just the body, offering entirely physical pleasure to any man. From here on out eroticism would include the panting after accomplishment and a throbbing for self-knowledge. Though it is often said that sexuality thrives in fantasy, here, now, it was well beyond fantasy. I was beckoning el curandero to enter the labyrinth of imagination, precisely the one he had opened up to me.

Now, I would lead him. I would give him back all he had forgotten, and everything he had lost in a trance would be restored. If there was a dead man, Suspicion, living inside of me, he would dissipate in the bright light of Macario's remembering.

With the dead man gone, I can enter a maze where I encounter a living partner on the other side of a trim, green hedge. He exists for me as real person with real-world love to give. Once again, there are two cups of coffee on the kitchen table, steam rising into the early sun. A simple hug on a comfortable couch. The extremes of romance and rape are no longer in my range of relationship.

Before Macario went home that night, we agreed to a farewell meeting at the park. I wanted to give him something, though not out of generosity. I had to be remembered. I took a taxi to the open market outside of town that sells everything from guitars to goat cheese. After considering leather wallets, jaguar masks, CDs of mood music, and a variety of baked goods, I came across a blank handmade book with the shape of a woman embossed on the cover. Perfect.

Back home I took the liberty of writing inside, "The first

woman I knew . . ." Maybe he'd write about me in the final pages. It would be a good ending—an account of the woman who had inspired him to write the book.

The park was especially wonderful that morning. The fountains gushed at full force, the skateboarders hurled themselves into the sky, and lovers sat on the benches, hugging and kissing as if no one else was there. I felt calm and relaxed at our final meeting. I held deep inside the vision of my future and realized that it did not include Macario or anyone like him. He may have been the cure, but he was not to be the answer.

"The first woman I knew . . ." He read it out loud and laughed.

I smiled back but could feel my mouth twisting in the wrong direction. Even though I was grateful to him, I didn't want to joke around. Polite but curt was the best I could manage. "Take care, Macario. Write your stories. When I return next year, I hope to read them."

He thanked me in the usual effusive way of a well-mannered Mexican. We hugged good-bye while he whispered, "Adios, Chica" directly into my ear.

I took a long last look at Macario's handsome face. He directed his gaze to my eyes. We stayed there for several seconds, then turned away and went in our separate directions. He had to give a massage at ten. I had to pack.

Filled with an unsettling ecstasy, I didn't sleep well that night before my departure. Sometimes I cried from happiness at the thought of what might come, sometimes from sadness because the future had not yet arrived. The strangeness of my experience with Macario lingered through the very early morning, until the wake-up alarm blasted all trace of unreality. When the airport shuttle arrived five minutes early, I yanked the suitcase handle and dragged both of us out the door.

Two hours later, I was settled alone in seat A on the 8:00 a.m. flight from Oaxaca.

16555858R00065

Made in the USA
San Bernardino, CA
09 November 2014